ROYAL LOVE

ALSO BY LARAMIE BRISCOE

The Haldonia Monarchy

Royal Rebel

Royal Chaos

ROYAL LOVE

A Haldonia Monarchy Novel

LARAMIE BRISCOE

LN
P

Royal Love
Paperback Edition
Copyright © 2025 by Laramie Briscoe

Love N. Books Press
An Imprint of Wolfpack Publishing
1707 E. Diana Street
Tampa, FL 33610

www.lovenbookspress.com

Cover Design by Jennilynn Wyer Designs
Edited by My Brother's Editor

Paperback ISBN 979-8-89567-122-1
Ebook ISBN 979-8-89567-121-4
LCCN 2025939829

ROYAL LOVE

ROYAL
LOVE

CHAPTER 1
TRISTAN

Happiness is fleeting. One minute you're ecstatic because the war is over, and your wife is pregnant. The next, you can't sleep through the night without the ravages of what you did appearing every time you close your eyes and fall into a deep sleep. You find yourself waking up screaming, your wife beside you, questioning what she can do, how she can help. But there's no help. There's nothing she can do, and you're stuck in a cycle of the things you did, the things you wanted to do, and the things you had to do.

That's where I find myself two months after the end of the war and discovering that Amelia is pregnant. Parker comes in through the side door of my office. "Sir, we need to leave. You have a public appearance."

I look up at him. "Has it been checked? All ways that someone could try and harm me have been checked, right?"

He calmly agrees, nodding. "Yes, Tristan, you're safe, I promise."

This was never an issue before the war, before people tried to take me out, and before I realized just how precious life can be. Does Parker have these fears? The ones that wake me up at night and leave me in a pool of sweat? "I have no doubt about that. I trust you."

"It's not about trust. You and I both know that. It's about how you feel." He raises his eyebrows. "How are you feeling?"

I run a hand through my hair. "When will I stop looking for it? The danger. When will I sleep through the night without waking up screaming? I don't expect you to have all the answers, I just need to know someone else is having problems with it too."

He glances over at me. "I'm having them too. Things aren't as great as they appear to be. That's a promise, Tristan. The only difference between us is I have a job to do that requires keeping you safe, which means I can compartmentalize."

I wish I had a way to do that, but all I can seem to think about is the future. A future I wasn't sure I'd have when I was in that tent with Parker. "Well, that makes me feel better, at least."

"So believe me when I say I've covered all the bases. You don't have to worry. No one is going to harm you on my watch."

There's nothing else I want more than to believe him. "All right then, let's get going."

* * *

The streets of Haldonia are packed as we make our way into the center of town. Kids are holding up signs, and the adults have looks of hope. I want that hope, but when I close my eyes, all I can see is the devastation around us every day we were fighting Crona.

Parker sits beside me. "We'll be in and out within thirty minutes, unless you decide to talk to your subjects personally."

I nod, barely hearing what he's saying. My heart is pounding, there's a feeling of doom in my stomach, and saliva starts overproducing in my mouth. If I'm not careful, I'm going to lose what I ate for breakfast. Closing my eyes, I concentrate on my breathing. "Sounds good, I'll do my best to be in and out."

"You don't have to hurry, you know. If there's a reason for you to be there, then I'll make sure you're safe." Parker turns to face me. "The thing that sets you apart from the leaders who came before you is how close you are to the people you rule. You've never been the type of man, much less leader, who doesn't listen to what they have to say.

Whether it takes five minutes or thirty. You're the type of man who will stay and listen."

Clearing my throat, I shake my head. "I'm not sure I'm that type of man any longer. The war changed me."

"It changed all of us," Parker reminds me. "We've got to figure out how to live with the people we were, and the people we are now."

And that's just it. I can't seem to reconcile the Tristan I was before I went into the war, and the one who came out. I'm not the same, I'm nowhere near close, and at some point, I'm going to have to admit that publicly. As I do that, will it invite others to attempt to invade us? That's what keeps me up at night. "You're right, and I'm doing the best I can."

My gaze cuts out the window. The day is gorgeous, full of sun and blue skies. It's warm, and the scent of the new season is on the breeze. I should be excited, but I feel so fucking empty. When the Range Rover comes to a stop, I rub my sweaty palms on my thighs and prepare to exit the vehicle.

"I'll come around and get you," Parker advises. "Same way we always do this. It's not changing just because we're out in public."

I nod, waiting for the door to open. When it does, I stutter slightly, not letting my feet touch the ground. For just a moment, I look at the sky and then touch my finger to my palm before inhaling deeply. The anxiety starts to dissipate slightly, and I'm thankful. Getting all the way out, I wave to everyone, taking their cheers into my chest and holding them tight. When things get too hard, I remember the people of Haldonia love me, and right now that has to be enough.

Walking up to the podium, I give a smile and speak from the heart. "We'll get through this, and we'll get through it together…"

CHAPTER 2
AMELIA

Tristan isn't happy. He's not sleeping well, and he seems to think he's hiding it from me. Today, I'm going through the motions, doing everything I'm supposed to do as the queen of Haldonia. Looking through all the invitations and letters that have been sent to me.

It's grown exponentially since the war.

So many of our younger citizens are looking toward me. Because of those addresses I gave every day. They want me to tell them that life will be better if they just stay the course.

The problem is, I can't believe that completely this time. Not after what I saw during the war. Not after what I've witnessed from my husband since he came home.

"How are you doing?"

I lift my head up to where Shannon is standing in the doorway. She's been a steady influence since we met, and there's no doubt in my mind she will continue to be. Her friendship kept me from going crazy, and I'll always count her as one of the most important people to me. "I'm okay. Tired. Which I've heard is to be expected. So far, I'm not puking, so we'll take that for as long as we can get it."

"Have you given any more thought to what we talked about last week?" she asks, coming fully into the office and having a seat.

I do my best to avoid her as I move things around on my desk and then move them back. It's a nervous habit I've picked up since coming back into the office. When I don't want to do something, I start playing around with what's right in front of me. Trying to figure out a better display for them. It never changes because I always go back to the first setup I had. "A little. I know I'm supposed to use the same doctor and hospital that all the other women in my situation have used, but what's going to happen if the hospital isn't ready for me?"

"I'm sure they're going to make sure it's prepared for you. You're the queen, after all."

That's part of the problem. I don't feel like a queen, and I don't feel like I'm helping my husband in the way he needs me to be. Not to mention, there are so many people in the country who've had their lives ripped apart. What makes me more special than they are? I'm struggling with that. Although I know I did all I could, it's still uncomfortable. "I am, but I'm having problems accepting the fact that I'm different than they are. That they expect me to take a spot another woman might need. My whole life I knew I was supposed to be the queen of Haldonia. At the time, I knew there were perks, but I didn't expect them this way." I swallow roughly.

Shannon reaches forward, grabbing my forearm in her hand. "There are always going to be people who think that you're given special treatment. And you are because of who you are. However, you can't let that stop you from getting what you need."

"So just because I was born at the right time, to the correct family, I got lucky."

"You did." She leans in. "None of us know what our circumstances are, what they're going to be, or how we're going to deal with them. You've been steadfast during all of this. There were many times when you could've decided you would hide. No one would have thought badly of you had you decided to do that. Can I be frank?"

"Yes, please. There aren't a whole lot of people I can speak to about any of this. You know I trust you."

"Survivor's guilt can be crippling. I'm not here to diagnose you or tell you how to feel, but what I am here to tell you, is the country is looking to you. They're not thinking about how you're getting preferential treatment. They're thinking about how this child you're carrying is going to be the light at the end of this dark tunnel. Your pregnancy might as well be the country's pregnancy, because everyone is excited about it. As they should be. You were able to keep us all from going crazy during those dark nights, and now you deserve some happiness. If the country wants to be a part of that, I say let them."

Her words hit me right in the chest. Is she right? Some of the women who lost everything are going to be happy for me. Not because I am who I am, but because they want to be a part of life continuing. We all need something to look forward to, and maybe this is what Haldonia needs. "Okay." I reach down, cupping the stomach that's not exactly there yet. "Then I'll accept it with the grace and gratitude it deserves."

"Good because you deserve it, too."

Looking at everything on my desk, I grin over at her. "Not to change the subject, but I have more requests than I know what to do with. I need some help to figure out what to do first." I've always valued her opinion, and since the war, I admire her even more than before. "Can you help me with that? Now that I know what you were actually hired for, I'm not sure whether you really enjoy these tasks, but you're good at them."

She grins as she has a seat beside me and scoots in. "Let's see what you have. There are some things I think should take precedent over others. The younger people of Haldonia feel a kinship to you because of the daily addresses you gave. They're kind of a forgotten aspect in this war, too, since their parents came home. I've been keeping up with some of the ones who were regular commenters on your videos. As much as they needed you through the war, they need someone like you now. It's almost as if you're the mother of the country."

My chest is heavy with the weight of that responsibility. "Do you really think they're looking at me that way?"

"Yeah." She nods. "It's a lot of pressure, I know, but you're a source of hope for everyone."

Everyone except my husband. I wish he looked at me that way, wish he could tell me how to help him. For the last week, he's awakened during the middle of the night, screaming. There's a sorrow in his eyes. The depths of it, I know I'll never understand. "Thanks, I'll keep all this in mind. I appreciate you, Shannon."

She wrinkles her nose. "Hey, we gotta stick together."

That we do. As she leaves, I start looking back through the requests that have been made for my time and make a few notes about who I would be willing to meet with. But when I hear my husband walking down the hallway, I hold my breath as I wonder if he'll come through my door or go to his office.

More than anything, I wish he'd come to mine, and we could have an afternoon like we had before the war started.

CHAPTER 3
TRISTAN

I'm exhausted. The toll it takes on me mentally and physically to be in the public eye is huge. Although I wish I could hide it, and I like to think I do, I know I don't. But only a few people see it or at least acknowledge it.

"What are your plans for the rest of the afternoon? We didn't talk about it this morning," Parker says as he enters my office and closes the door.

"Lia and I will be having dinner, and that's probably about it."

"You'll be having dinner here?"

Reaching up, I loosen my tie and swallow roughly. I know there are a bunch of local restaurants that would love to see us, but I know I won't be able to relax. There are too many variables I'm not able to control, and I don't want to be the person who requests the entire place be closed for me. While I do very much have that right, I'm aware of how it looks coming out of the situation we were just in. "Yeah, we're having dinner here."

"All right, then I'll leave you two alone. Would you like to go up to the beach house this weekend?"

It's not very often Parker makes that suggestion as it's more work for him, but if he's suggesting it, then it's obvious I'm having a hard time adjusting. God, I wish I could hide all of the shit going through my head from everyone, but there are people who know me well. I should be blessed by it, but right now I see it as a hindrance. "Let me talk to Lia. I'd love it, but I want to make sure she's on the same page as me."

He pulls up the sleeve of his suit jacket and checks his watch. "What time are you planning on clocking out tonight?"

When I glance at the clock on my desk, it reads three p.m. Typically I'm here for three more hours, but I've had enough for the day. Being out in public, like I was earlier, takes a lot out of me. "I think I'm going to go see what Lia's doing and head out."

His eyebrows go up, and he nods, but he doesn't say anything to give away his surprise. "Then I'll make sure that you all make it to the residential side and then check out for the night myself. You know where I am, if you need me."

I do. I make it a habit to know where he is. In case there's a chance I might need help, or Lia might need a quick getaway, I need to know where he and Shannon are at all times. I'm not sure I'll ever get over that. It's not the most comfortable thing in the world to constantly be thinking of a getaway, but I'm starting to accept this is who I am now. Things changed the moment Haldonia got bombed, and I'm not sure they'll ever go back to what they were before. I mean, I'm not sure they're supposed to. It's something I've been thinking about a lot lately. There are moments that affect your entire life. They may be five seconds or five months, but they can stop you in your tracks and change the trajectory of everything. A word someone says, a global pandemic, or war. It's life-changing, and trying to figure out who you are after that change? It's not easy. In fact, it's one of the hardest things I've ever had to do. Getting up, I throw a smile at Parker. It doesn't reach my eyes, and I know it. Not many have for the last few weeks, and I leave my office, heading for Lia's.

When I get there, I knock, waiting for her voice.

"You may enter."

It's all so proper, and I hate how I didn't just walk in. The me from a few months ago would've just walked in and to hell with the conse-quences. "Hey," I say as I walk in, and then stop a few feet inside.

Putting my hands in the pockets of my slacks, I rock back on my heels. Nerves dance in my stomach, so different from what it was in the before times.

"Hey yourself." Her smile is so bright I can see it from across the room. "You're here early." She glances down at the clock.

"Yeah." I reach back and grasp the doorframe with my hands, holding on so that I don't reach out and grab her. If I touch her, then I might not be able to keep it together. "Decided it was over with for the day. I don't know about you, but I'm hungry. Thought we could go have dinner earlier than normal, then spend some time together." That hadn't been my original idea, but as soon as I saw her sitting there behind her desk, those plans changed. It's been too long since I cuddled her and took a few minutes to relax. It's as if I've been in a constant state of fight or flight. My heart hasn't had a prolonged amount of time to rest, and I can feel it in the tightness of my chest.

Her cheeks flush pink, giving her the look of pleasure. Back before I was drug into the situation with Crona, I saw this all the time—her looking at me with a secret smile, a twinkle in her eyes, and the knowledge that we'd be having a good time together in a few short hours. The trauma I suffered, and her too, has changed all of that. I'm trying to get it back, but I have no idea if I'm even skimming the surface.

"That sounds great to me," she finally answers. "I have a couple of things I need to do, and then I'll be ready to go. Fifteen minutes?" She raises her eyebrows.

I don't want to go back to my office and be alone. I'm craving being next to her, not being by myself. Maybe this means I'm starting to turn a corner because I've had my fair share of wanting to be a loner since we came home. It's all I can hope for.

CHAPTER 4
AMELIA

I'm surprised when Tristan comes to the door and then walks through it. He hasn't done this in longer than I care to admit. I've been doing my best not to impose my thoughts about how he should be handling the big feelings he must have on him, but this gives me some hope.

"Mind if I stay while you finish up?" he asks.

This surprises me even more, and I do my best to keep it off my face. "You can stay with me anytime. You never have to ask." Now I wish I hadn't told Shannon I would finish a few of the tasks to get us started in the morning.

My eyes track him as he leans back against the cushions of the couch and spreads his legs out, lying down. I had hoped when he came back from war, those dark circles would go away under his eyes. That was one of my biggest hopes and prayers for him. That after being on for so long he would be able to relax and catch up on sleep. Now I realize how naïve that was. I should've anticipated he would have issues, but I didn't, and now I don't know how to help him. His eyes are closed, dark eyelashes kissing his cheeks, but behind those eyelids, he isn't restful. There's movement, and his legs are twitching. Quickly, I hurry to finish up what I've been working on.

When I'm finished, I get up and do my best to make as much noise as possible crossing the room. I've learned how bad it can be to wake Tristan up without him knowing you're there. When I get close, his eyes pop open, and he stares at me like he doesn't recognize me. "Tris, it's me, Lia. Do you know where you are?" This is another part I've learned. I have to make sure he knows who I am. Assuming can be dangerous.

He looks around, like he doesn't recognize my office, and then it seems to hit him. "Did I fall asleep?" His voice is full of deep gravel, and the sound runs over my arms.

"You did. I know you're tired." I reach out to him, running my fingers through his hair. "You're not sleeping well at night, so I know you need to be getting it where you can."

His eyes shutter. "I'm doing the best I can, Lia. It's not been easy."

"I know." I reach out, grabbing his hand with mine. "I wish there was something I could do for you."

"What is it you want to do for me?" he asks in a tone I don't love. It's almost accusatory.

"Whatever I can to make this easier. You're my husband, the father of my child." I reach down, cupping my barely there bump. "More than anything, I want you to be okay."

"I don't know if I'll ever be okay," he admits.

And that's a truth I'm going to have to accept. I can't force him to blindly tell me he's good when he isn't. That's not what marriage is, as much as I would like for it to be. "We're going to figure this out. No matter how long it takes. We'll have the life we wanted, Tris."

He presses his lips together in a firm line. "I wish I could believe you, babe. But right now, it just doesn't seem possible.

"I know, and I'll keep the faith alive for both of us." I have to because I won't let us become a statistic, I refuse to let us fail. From the moment I walked into the room next door and was introduced to Tristan, I knew he was my future. I won't let him go because things aren't easy. Marriage is work, and we'll figure it out.

As we make our way to the main living area of the castle, he holds my hand tightly. It makes me wonder if it's for him or for me. Regardless, it feels good for his strong warmth to be wrapped around my smaller and colder hand.

"How are you feeling?" he asks, his deep voice reverberating off the sides of the hallway.

At one point right after we'd first gotten married, these hallways were full of people, voices, and laughter. That changed the moment the building was rocked by enemy fire. If I close my eyes, I can still remember what it felt like that day. The fear, the uncertainty, the way I'd reached for Tristan's hand, and he'd been right there. Although I had been scared, I hadn't been worried. Somehow, I'd known that Tristan would protect me, even when he should've protected himself first.

"I'm good," I answer. "So far not a whole lot of nausea and no getting sick." I give him a small smile.

He answers with one of his own. It's been so long since I've seen one spread across his face and overtake his eyes, that I reach out and grasp it with my fingers, holding it close to my heart.

"Would you tell me if you have been feeling sick? I haven't been a supportive partner lately, and I'm sorry."

Rolling my lips together, I end by pulling the bottom one in between my teeth. The nerves in my stomach dance as I contemplate what I want to say. There's a lot of pressure. What if I say the wrong thing? What if I say the right thing? There's no guarantee Tristan will take either of the things I'm trying to say as good or bad. Since he came back from the battlefield, he takes things differently than he used to. I don't know this man nearly as well as I knew the man before he left. "You haven't been *not* supportive. It's hard for both of us."

A frustrated sigh escapes his chest. "I'm trying to figure out why it's been so hard. We won, our country is recovering, and we're continuing the line of succession. Everything here should be good. We should be happy."

Grabbing his hand, I pull him to the left, through a hallway, into a room. It's the room where we first met each other on my first night at the castle. When we step in and close the door, it's as if we've been transported right back there. I'm taken back to the same unsure woman I was, but I don't let the uncertainty overtake me. Instead, I go to the couch and motion for him to sit down. When he does, I stand in front of him and tilt my head to the side. "You know what you need? A drink. One like you poured us the first night we were here."

He nods, agreeing.

It's been a while since I've been able to take care of him. Walking over to the bar on unsteady heels, I take a moment to center myself. It's surreal to be back here, with my husband, carrying our child, after everything we've been through. Taking a deep breath through my nose and then out my mouth, I prepare his drink before turning and walking back over to him.

"Here ya go."

"Thank you."

Immediately, he takes a drink, and I have a seat across from him. Licking my lips, I start. "You said something back there. We should be happy. I am, are you?"

"It's not that I'm not happy," he starts. "It's that I can't get over what I did out there on the battlefield in the name of my country." His voice is so low, I almost can't hear him.

"Why don't you tell me about some of it? Let me help you with what you are dealing with."

He runs a hand through his hair. "I'm just not sure I can."

CHAPTER 5
TRISTAN

I squeeze her hand, feeling the warmth seep into my skin. It's cold with the realization of everything I've done. "Lia, it's not you. It's me." The words sound cliché, even to my own ears, but they're true. How do I make her understand the weight I carry? The guilt I'm assaulted with every time I allow myself to think about what I've done?

Her eyes soften, and she shifts closer, her presence a balm to my racing heart. "Tristan, you don't have to ask for forgiveness."

I flinch, her words slicing through my defenses. Voice hoarse, I continue. "But I do, Lia. For so much."

She shakes her head, firm yet gentle. Those eyes of hers are soft and hard at the same time. "No, you don't. What you did was about survival. It wasn't about right or wrong in the way we normally think of it. You did the most important thing of all—you survived."

The breath catches in my throat, and suddenly the air feels heavier than it has before. "Survived," I spit the word out, hating the taste of it.

"Yes," she insists. "And surviving sometimes means making impossible choices. Choices that none of us can fully understand unless we've been there."

"But I took lives, Lia," I confess, the admission a stone dropping into a still pond. Those ripples are sure to bother others, and I'm scared to death about when I'm called to answer for my transgressions.

Her grip on my hand tightens. "And it wasn't without a cost to you. I see that. But you need to understand something, Tristan. Sometimes, the act of surviving is the bravest thing of all."

I blink, trying to absorb her words. Could surviving really be an act of bravery, rather than a stain on my soul? It's not like my soul has been pristine. I've done shit that others shouldn't forgive. I've been so focused on my own failures that I haven't considered the possibility.

Amelia lifts my chin, forcing me to meet her gaze with her soft fingers. "I carried my own burdens, Tristan. Public appearances, speeches, playing the part. None of it came naturally to me, but I learned. It was necessary. You're going to have to learn."

I nod slowly, the pieces beginning to fit together in my mind. Her battles were fought in the public eye, mine in the shadows. Different situations, same war.

"It still feels like I failed," I whisper, the truth clawing its way out of my hoarse throat.

"You didn't fail." Her voice is steady, reminding me, just like my mom used to. "You adapted. You did what you had to do, and that's a success in its own right."

I want to believe her. I want to shed this too-tight skin of self-doubt that clings to me. "But how do I move forward, knowing the things I've done?"

Her smile is sad, understanding. "One step at a time. We don't erase the past, Tristan. We learn to carry it with us, like a shadow. It's part of who we are, but not all of it."

And those words are what I hang on to as I reach forward, wrapping my arms around her waist, needing to hold on to her tightly as I try to take that first step.

CHAPTER 6
AMELIA

Although it shouldn't bother me, being out among the people, it does. In ways I never imagined once the war was over. The people have requested I be at more public gatherings than ever, and while that wouldn't have bothered me before, it does now.

Shannon glances over at me from where she sits in the seat opposite. "Are you okay? It looks like you're about to lose your breakfast."

Truth be told, I am. Morning sickness hasn't been awful for me since I got pregnant, but when I have situations where I must be awake and ready for early, it starts to mess with me. Then there's the threat of being in front of the people. While many of them thought it was good that I would make daily addresses, there were an equal number who saw Haldonia as aggressors because we dropped bombs, just like Crona did. "Yeah, worried that there's going to be protests," I admit.

"If there are, we'll deal with it."

That's easy for her to say because not everyone looks for her to make a statement. They don't expect her to come out and be one with the people. To be fair, she isn't in that type of role, but I'm not sure anyone will ever be able to understand, besides Tristan.

As we pull up to the event I've been invited to, a crowd has already formed. Nerves cause my stomach to roll, especially as I see there is a group of people there with protest signs.

The signs are bold and angry, vivid colors screaming for attention. Words like "Warmonger!" and "Peace Now!" clash against each other, creating a sea of conflicting emotions. I take a deep breath, trying to steady myself.

"All right, let's do this," I say, more to myself than to Shannon. She gives me a reassuring nod, and we step out of the car. The air is cool, a gentle breeze weaving through the crowd. The noise is a mix of chants from the protesters and cheers from those who have gathered to support me.

As I make my way to the stage, I see the faces of those who've come hoping for words of reassurance. There are families, young people, and elders—all looking at me with expectation. I pause for a moment, letting their energy wash over me, grounding me in the present. They need hope. I need to be that hope.

The protesters' voices rise in volume. I can hear fractions of their chants penetrating the hum of the supporters. It would be easy to get lost in that sound, to let my anxiety take root, but I refuse. Instead, I focus on the people who've come seeking something only I can give—peace of mind, a promise of a better future.

I step up to the podium, the microphone catching my breath before I've even spoken. The crowd quiets down, anticipation vibrating in the air. I clear my throat, my heart hammering in my chest. This is it. This is why I'm here.

"Thank you all for being here today," I begin, my voice steady and strong, even as the protesters' chants linger at the edges. "We stand here not just as citizens of Haldonia, but as members of a world reshaped by struggle, pain, and ultimately, hope."

The words flow, a river of acknowledgment for the past and a beacon for the future. I focus on the families in front of me, some holding small flags, others with joined hands—a tapestry of unity despite the turmoil.

"We have seen darkness," I continue, "and we have felt despair. But in that darkness, each of you has become a spark, a light that refuses to be extinguished."

A small cheer rises, and I see nods of agreement. My confidence builds, born from their reaction, their belief in my words.

"The world is watching us, questioning every move, every decision. And while we cannot erase the scars of yesterday, we can choose to build a tomorrow defined not by fear, but by courage."

I pause, letting the words settle. The protesters' chants are loud, insistent, but they are not my focus. My gaze sweeps across the crowd, catching eyes filled with tears, determination, and something else—hope.

"Haldonia will not forget," I say, voice ringing clear. "We will honor those who fought and those who fell, by working tirelessly to rebuild, to heal, and to stand tall once more. Together, we shall cultivate a legacy of peace."

A wave of applause crashes over me, the sound buoying my spirits. This is why I'm here. For them. For this moment of unity amid the chaos.

"As long as we hold on to each other, as long as we believe in our collective strength, we will find a way forward. We are more than our past actions. We are the architects of our future."

The energy shifts subtly, a palpable change, as the chorus calling for peace intertwines with my message, finding common ground. The protesters are quieter now, some even lowering their signs, their expressions softening as they listen.

"We must strive for understanding," I urge, glancing briefly toward the protesters, acknowledging their presence. "It's only through open hearts and open minds that we can bridge the divide that separates us."

The murmurs of agreement ripple back to me, and I feel something spark, a connection weaving among us all.

"Haldonia is strong, not because of its power, but because of its people—each and every one of you." I pause, letting my gaze settle on individual faces, young and old. "Let us continue to stand together, to support one another, and to be the change we wish to see in the world."

The applause that follows is thunderous, an overwhelming response that swells my heart with pride and gratitude. I step back from the microphone, letting their energy wash over me, a reminder of why I lead, why I speak.

One voice, a young woman, calls out from the crowd, "We believe in you, Amelia!"

Others echo her sentiment, a chant of support rising up like a clarion call.

As I step down from the stage, Shannon is there, offering a supportive smile. "You did great," she says, her voice laced with genuine warmth.

I nod, the weight of the moment still settling on my shoulders. "Thank you," I whisper, knowing that today was just one of many battles for the soul of our nation.

The protesters still linger at the edges, holding their signs, their expressions less confrontational now. I walk toward them, feeling an impulse to reach out, to extend that olive branch.

"Thank you for being here," I say, meeting their eyes, allowing myself to be vulnerable, open. "Your voices are important—let's use them to build something beautiful."

A few of them nod, and I see a flicker of understanding pass between us. It's a start.

I turn back to the crowd, seeing faces alight with newfound hope. For a moment, I close my eyes, capturing this feeling of unity, of purpose.

This is not just a speech, it's a promise. A promise I intend to keep, with every beat of my heart and every breath in my body. Together, we will shape the future. Together, we are unstoppable.

CHAPTER 7
TRISTAN

I am so fucking proud of my wife. Watching the live stream is a test of patience. There's nothing I want more than to go to her as I see the protesters have shown up, but this is her time to shine. Just like it was she who brought everyone together during the war.

"She and Shannon look like they have this," Parker notes as he sits next to me.

"They're composed. Much more than I have been lately."

Parker chuckles. "The thing most people don't talk about is coming back from war. They always say how happy they are to be home, how nice it is to not be out on the battlefield anymore, but they don't talk about the hard shit." He runs a hand through his hair. "You know I come from a military background. I've been in situations like what we were in previously. Coming home was always a bit of a mindfuck. On one hand, you're so excited not to be on the edge anymore. You're grateful to be eating great food, sleeping in a real bed, and not having to watch your back. At the same time, you're trying to come to grips with what you did out there. Is that where you are?"

Licking my lips, I nod. "Yeah. I'm having nightmares about some of the shit we saw, but I'm also feeling fucking guilty. Why should we have survived and others not? What was the difference between us and them? Why am I considered better? There were men and women standing with us who had kids and families at home, and they're never going to see those loved ones again. How do I deal with that?"

"The best way you can. There's no guidebook, Tristan. You're the face and heart of this country. People will be looking to you to see how they handle life as it begins again. If you aren't sure you can handle it, you might want to admit that to yourself and be honest with the people." He runs a hand across his jaw, sighing heavily. "If you don't feel it, they're going to see it, and they may be worried that we're in a similar situation again. Believe it or not, I think you'll do more being honest than you will putting on a brave face."

I think about what Parker has said. "You're right about that, but you're wrong about something else."

"Oh yeah? What's that?"

"I might be the face of this country, but Lia's the fucking heart of it. They'll go to battle for her in ways they never even thought of for me."

A lesser man might think worse of their wife for having such a strong hold on his country, but I know how lucky I am. My mother was loved by the people, and all I've ever wanted is for those same people to love my wife just as much.

The livestream ends, and the room feels quieter, somehow smaller without her presence streaming in on the screen. I sink back into the couch, Parker's words lingering like remnants of the war we fucking fought.

Amelia has a way of making everyone around her feel seen—like each person she interacts with somehow becomes the most important person in the room. Watching her calm the protesters with grace and power only reaffirms what I constantly tell myself. I am the luckiest man alive. We were blessed to have the arranged marriage we do.

◆━━━◆━━●━━◆━━◆

An hour later, the door creaks open, and I turn instinctively. Amelia steps inside, still wearing the fitted navy dress she chose for today's event. It's tighter around her breasts than it was the last time she wore it, reminding me that she carries our child. Her hair is pulled back, with just a few tendrils framing her face. She pauses, takes a deep breath, and lets the door close softly behind her.

I stand, the urge to hold her overwhelming. There were so many times I wanted my arms around her when it wasn't physically capable of happening. I promised myself back then I would do it any time I wanted to moving forward. Crossing the room, I pull her into my embrace, breathing in her familiar scent. "You were brilliant," I whisper, pressing a gentle kiss to her temple.

Amelia leans into me for just a moment, allowing her body to relax, before pulling back and meeting my gaze. "It was intense, but we managed." Her eyes are filled with a mix of relief and determination.

"I'm so proud of you," I tell her, brushing my thumb across her cheek, before dropping a kiss there. It's slightly awkward, as we haven't found our groove yet, from being apart. "You're incredible, you know that?"

She arches a brow, a teasing smile tugging at her lips. "Oh? And here I thought I was just the queen."

"You're more than just the queen." I bend down so that our foreheads meet. "The way you handled today, Amelia...it was sexy as hell." I can't help but grin, the playful admiration in my words genuine. One of the first times I've felt like smiling since all of this started.

A laugh escapes her, and her tension visibly eases. "Well, I suppose managing a monarchy comes with its perks."

I draw her back into a hug, feeling the weight of the day release between us. This is what I wanted so many times when it was just Parker and I trying to stay alive. "You make it look damn good."

Her expression softens, and she meets my eyes with a sincerity that never fails to ground me. "And you make it worth it. No matter how scared I was to meet you and become your wife, you've always made it worth it."

We stand together, wrapped in each other. Everything Parker and I went through plays over and over in my head, forcing me to swallow hard, trying to forget the sacrifice I made for the people.

"Are you ready to talk about it?" she asks, always in tune with how I'm feeling.

Her question hangs between us, a gentle prompt that I know is rooted in love, but there's so much darkness attached to it. I hesitate, searching for the words and feeling the weight of responsibility.

"Some of it," I confess finally. "I'm trying to find the balance between being honest with our people and not wanting to worry them."

Amelia nods, understanding etched into every line of her face. She squeezes my waist. "Tristan, they trust you because you're real with them. We're in this together, and they know it. We just have to remind them that it's okay to not have all the answers right away."

Her faith in me is fucking amazing. It's what gets me through. "You always know what to say to make me feel…more myself."

"That's because you are yourself." She smiles, the gesture a bit shy. "Just as much as I'm myself when I'm with you."

Her confidence wraps around us, and it's everything I need in this moment. I know there's no guidebook for any of this, but we're making our own, page by page, together. It's messy and real, full of all the truth we can manage, even when it's uncomfortable.

Amelia steps back, her fingers brushing against mine as she heads for the small table in the room. She pours a glass of water and a scotch before returning to my side. She hands me the scotch.

"To us," she offers simply, raising her glass.

"To us," I echo, clinking my glass against hers.

We drink, the warmth spreading through me, both from the alcohol and being near her. Her presence takes away the stress of the day, the tense reality I live with now. Still, my leg shakes, knee bouncing with unrestrained nerves.

"What do you say we take a walk in the garden?" she suggests, raising an eyebrow.

I nod, grateful for her understanding without me having to say it. This garden was my mother's pride and joy, more than anything I want to share it with her. "I'd love that." I take her hand, and we make our way outside, the cool air a soothing balm as we step into what's turned into early evening.

The garden paths, illuminated by soft lanterns, are a refuge I feel like we're going to make good use of since we're back in town. It can be a place where titles melt away, and everything turns into just Tristan and Amelia.

We walk in silence, peace settling over us. I stop, turning to face her. "You are as beautiful now as the day I first saw you."

She chuckles, the sound dances in the air. It's this that I thought about in the worst moments, reminding me that there was laughter before all the devastation. "That feels like a lifetime ago."

"Some days, it feels like just yesterday."

She moves closer, her fingers intertwining with mine. "And here we are." Her eyes search mine.

I wish I knew what she was looking for. "Here we are," I repeat, not liking the quietness between us.

Amelia reaches up, her fingers brushing against my cheek. "Whatever comes, we'll face it together," she states, her words a promise that I pray she'll never renege on.

I tug her gently toward me, our foreheads touching. "Together," I agree, my voice a soft echo of hers, packed with unspoken promises and shared dreams. Hoping against everything that I can take those dark moments at night and shove them into a locked compartment within myself.

In the garden's quiet embrace, we make our way back toward the castle, hand in hand. The future, though uncertain, doesn't intimidate me with her by my side. Not right now, doesn't mean it won't in the next five minutes, but for now, I'm okay. Inside, the warmth greets us once more, a vibrant contrast to the night outside. Amelia pauses at the doorway, looking up at me with a radiant smile that seems to hold the world in its curve.

"Are you hungry?" she asks, tilting her head slightly, her gaze playful yet sincere.

I consider her question for a moment. "I could eat," I admit, realizing how true it is in every sense. My stomach growls, and my cock swells against the zipper of my pants.

We head to the kitchen, where the noise of the workers in the kitchen reminds me of being a kid. It's one of those moments where I can almost imagine my mom walking through the door and asking me if I'm excited for dinner. Especially when I see what we're having.

Spaghetti, something simple and familiar, sits here waiting for us to eat it.

We take a seat at the table, and together, we have one of the best dinners I've had since I came home. When we're done, she glances at me, her eyes hot and heavy. "Are you ready for bed, Tris?"

Fuck yeah, I am.

CHAPTER 8
TRISTAN

As soon as we step over the threshold of our bedroom, I'm pressing her against the opposite wall. Dropping my mouth to her shoulder, my voice is low as I speak to her. "I've thought about having you naked and beneath me most of the day. I know you've not been feeling the best, so I need to know what you're into tonight."

Her eyebrows rise. "No matter how sick I am, I always want you."

Running my knuckles across her cheek, I dip down and whisper. "Doesn't matter to me either way. My cock always wants you, too."

"Okay." She nods, swallowing roughly. "I respect that."

"Thanks, because I'm about to totally disrespect you."

She snorts, but it turns into a moan as I reach around and grip her neck, not hard, just enough so that she knows I'm there. Tonight I feel like making a claim on her. So much of her is given to the people of Haldonia, and tonight, I need to know she's mine. "Tristan…"

"Too much?" I question, ready to reel it back in if need be.

"Just enough, but I want out of these clothes, and I know you do too."

She's right. I turn her around and hitch her up so that she can wrap her legs around my waist. It's hard, since her belly is slightly in the way, but I make it work. Walking us back to the bedroom, I set her down, and then before I know it, we're both naked. Slow-rolling over to her, I hook my hand around her waist and pull her in for a kiss. Our tongues tangle, our breath mingles, and I shove my fingers through her hair, holding her tightly to me.

We tumble onto the bed, and I press myself up into a push-up over her, making sure to keep my belly off hers. Pulling my mouth back from hers, I drop it down to her nipple, worrying the hard nub with my lips and teeth. She moans, digging her nails into my flesh.

"That feels so good, Tris."

I groan my agreement and hold the base of my cock in my hand, rubbing the head of it against the hood of her clit. She's wet and getting wetter by the second as I replace the head with my fingers. She's tight as fuck, as she always is for me. I use my fingers to stretch her, preparing for my invasion.

We writhe against one another, trying to quench the thirst between us. Her hand slips down my stomach, grabbing hold of my cock, jacking it up and down. "Holy fuck." I tilt my head back as her hand works me. "I hope you're as ready for me as I am for you."

"I am," she moans, her wetness coating my fingers. Since she got pregnant, she's been ready for me at all times.

She follows me with her grip as I pop off the bed with one leg, ready to get enough leverage. When I do, she grabs hold of my thighs and pulls me to her.

Together, we work my cock inside her, moaning as I slide fully in. It's on from here. We're thrusting and moving against one another, rubbing parts of our body. Her fingers rake the skin of my chest, I use my fingers to tighten the nub of her breast. Her mouth opens as I lean down and take that nub in my teeth, yanking as hard as I dare.

"Fucking hell, Tris," she pants, her legs falling further open. "You keep doing that, I'm going to come, and I'm going to come quick."

I take that as a personal challenge. With a one-track mind, I continue doing just that as her pussy tightens around my cock. Out of nowhere, she grabs hold of my hair and yanks as she comes in rolling waves. That's all I need to fly over the edge with her.

As we're trying to get our breath back, she nuzzles against my chest. "I don't know what got into you, but I'd like it more often."

I laugh. "Me neither, but sometimes I need you more than I need my next breath."

She closes her eyes and tilts her forehead to mine. This is everything I need in my life, right here.

CHAPTER 9
AMELIA

I've not felt as close to Tristan as I do in this moment after he's taken me to heaven and back. This is who I want us to be, who I imagined we would be when we got married. But life had other plans. We were thrust into a war—not of our own making—and it was all about survival.

And I should be exhausted, especially after what we've been through the last few months, but I'm not. Instead, I'm staring at my husband. Right this second is the most at peace he's looked since he came home. With my fingers, I reach up and run them through his hair, scratching at his scalp.

Eventually that peaceful look starts being replaced.

My stomach cramps as I watch it. Gone is the calm, and in its place is something I can't actually put my finger on.

Tristan's face screws up in what appears to be either fear or pain. Reaching up, I push against the skin of his forehead in between his eyebrows, smoothing the lines. "It's okay," I soothe softly. "You're okay."

But that doesn't soothe him, not in the way I want it too. Instead of resting, his head starts shaking back and forth on the pillow. Sounds escape from his chest, ones that are savage in their intensity and panicky in the way he's trying to get air into his lungs.

"No…" he screams. "Don't go over there. You don't have any cover!"

"Tristan, you're not there anymore. You're here with me. It's okay," I croon.

That's when a hand wraps around my wrist, fingers hanging on tightly. "Don't touch me."

The voice. It's not Tristan's. It's someone else who I don't know. Full of harshness, and severity. I've never heard this tone from him before. It causes icy fear to wash over me. "Tris, it's me. It's Lia, your wife. You know me."

With a cry, he flips me over, holding my wrists above my head. I'm doing my best not to be frightened, but I've never seen this look in his eyes before. It's as if he hates me, as if he could chew me up and spit me out, or break me in half. Never before have I felt unsafe with him, but my heart is pounding in my chest, sweat has bloomed on every part of my body, and I'm terrified what he may do. "You're not going to kill me." He grits through his teeth.

"No, I'm not," I say as calmly as possible. "I don't want to hurt you, and you don't want to hurt me."

His eyes are unfocused in a way I've never seen before, and I don't know how to make him snap out of it. Reaching up, he wraps his fingers around my throat, squeezing roughly. I begin beating on his back, trying to get him to loosen his hold. His forearm is in front of my mouth, and I manage to open my mouth and bite down as hard as I can.

When he lets go, I inhale deeply, giving my deprived lungs what they need, and scream loudly.

Before I can do anything else, the door busts open and here comes Parker and Shannon, both carrying. "What's happening?" he asks, as he comes over to where we are.

"Bad dream, and I can't get him out of it."

Parker makes a noise in the back of his throat and holsters his weapon before grabbing Tristan by his shoulders, yanking him off of me. Something about the motion snaps Tristan out of it, and when they're face-to-face, I hear a voice come out of my husband that I've never heard before.

"Oh my god, what did I do? Is she okay?"

Parker says something softly, but when Tristan looks up at me, the fear in those eyes is enough to make me cry. I hate this for him, for us, and I don't know how to fix it. Before I can say anything else, Tristan is on his feet and running for the door.

"Help him?" I beg Parker.

"I will." He nods and takes off at a run after him.

"Are you okay?" Shannon asks, coming over to where I lay with the cover pulled up over my bare breasts. "Did he hurt you?"

"No," I cry.

And in that moment, I sink into her arms, letting her hold me closely.

Her embrace is like a lifeline, grounding me when everything feels like it's flapping in the wind. Shannon's warmth seeps into my bones as I cling to her, my tears soaking into her shirt.

"I'm so afraid for him, Shan," I whisper, my voice trembling with a fear I can't quite explain. "He's in so much pain, and I don't know how to reach him. There's never been a point I've been scared of him until tonight."

Shannon pulls back slightly, tucking a strand of hair behind my ear with gentle fingers. Her eyes, soft but determined, meet mine. "We'll find a way, Amelia. You're not alone in this."

Her words are like a balm, offering a flicker of hope in the thick fog of despair. I nod, swallowing hard even as fresh tears spill over. "But how?" I ask, my voice barely a whisper. "How do we pull him out of this darkness when he won't even let me in?"

"We take it one day at a time," Shannon replies, her voice steady. "We hold him up with love and patience. He needs us to be strong, so we will be."

I nod again, trying to absorb her strength. It's as though she's handing me a piece of her resilience, allowing me to borrow it when I have none. I know Shannon means every word, and her belief awakens something in me that I thought was lost in these last few moments—determination.

"You're right," I murmur, wiping my cheeks. "We can't give up on him. Not now, not ever."

Shannon squeezes my hand, her presence both solid and comforting. "Exactly. We'll fight for him, Amelia. Together."

It's not a solution, but it's a start—a fragile thread of hope to cling to as we navigate through the consequences of the actions Parker and Tristan took while in the war.

I take a deep breath, steadying myself. "Okay," I say, my voice firmer now. "Okay. We'll find a way."

And I believe it. With every fiber of my being, I cling to the promise that we will find a way back to each other, back to peace, back to love, back to the life we were building before all of this exploded in our faces.

CHAPTER 10
TRISTAN

"Oh my god, what the fuck did I do? Parker, is she okay?" My voice isn't my own. It's tortured and full of fear. Not of the situation, but of myself. "I could've killed her."

"No, you wouldn't," Parker assures me. "You would never hurt her."

"I didn't think so either, but motherfucker, I woke up with my hand wrapped around her throat. Who the fuck am I?"

He wraps his hands around my wrists, forcing me to look at him. "You're a man trying to figure out your place in this world after you had to make horrible decisions," Parker says. "You need to give yourself some grace."

"Grace? I couldn't even give my wife a night without me having a breakdown."

Letting go of my wrists, he wraps his arms around my waist and holds on tightly. "You need help, Tristan. It won't hurt to ask for it."

His words linger in the air, a lifeline thrown into the dark waters I'm drowning in. Parker's embrace is steady, grounding, and I find myself leaning into it. The war was supposed to be over, but inside me, a new battle rages—one where I'm both the soldier and the enemy.

"I don't know how to stop this," I admit, my voice raw and barely a whisper. The nights are the worst, haunted by shadows of memories that refuse to fade. The terror that grips me isn't just of the past, but of bringing that chaos into our home, into our bed, where Lia should feel safe.

"It's okay to feel lost, Tristan," Parker murmurs against my ear. "But you don't have to navigate this alone. Real strength is knowing when to reach out for a hand."

I inhale slowly, the scent of him giving me some measure of relief. I smelled his body wash so often while we were in the tent together that now it's almost comforting to me. It reminds me that I'm here, not there. Yet, danger lurks in my mind's shadows, sneaking into dreams where they don't belong.

"How do I even start?" I ask, pulling back to search his eyes. They're filled with a mixture of understanding and determination, a mirror of what I should have but don't quite feel.

"We'll find someone together," Parker promises. "I'll be with you every step of the way. You're not alone in this, Tristan. When you're ready, you can invite Amelia into the process, but I'll make sure the person is vetted and you can trust them."

His sincerity touches something deep inside, a place I've kept under lock and key. Maybe it's fear that holds me back, but within that fear is the potential for hope. Maybe, just maybe, seeking help isn't a sign of weakness, but a path to reclaiming my life, making it mine again.

I nod, slow and reluctant at first, but with each motion, I feel a bit of weight lifting. "Okay," I whisper, my voice barely above the breeze that carries the promise of dawn through the open window. "Okay. I'll do it."

"We'll carry you through this, my king. The entire country and your family. We're here for you."

And for the first time I don't feel so alone.

CHAPTER 11
AMELIA

The clock on the nightstand reads 2:13 a.m. when I hear the bedroom door creak open. I don't turn around, though I've been awake since he stormed out three hours ago. The argument replays in my mind—his voice rising, my tearful accusations, and the slam of the door that made the palace walls seem to shudder.

The mattress dips as Tristan sits on the edge of the bed. I can feel his hesitation, the careful way he's trying not to disturb me though he must know I'm awake.

"Lia?" His voice is soft, tentative. So different from the king who commands rooms with his presence.

I roll over slowly, taking in his disheveled appearance—his usually perfect hair windswept, his shirt wrinkled. There's vulnerability in his eyes that makes my heart ache despite my lingering anger.

"I'm sorry," he whispers. "I shouldn't have run out like that."

I sit up against the headboard, pulling the sheets around me. My hand instinctively moves to the small swell of my four-month pregnant belly, a gesture that doesn't escape his notice.

"I've made a decision," he says after a moment of heavy silence. "I've been thinking about it for weeks, but after tonight...I know it's what I need to do."

I wait, giving him the space to find his words. This is something I've learned about loving Tristan—sometimes he needs silence to gather his thoughts.

"I'm going to start seeing Dr. Merrick. For counseling."

The confession hangs between us. Despite our earlier fight, I feel a swell of pride and love so intense it takes my breath away.

"Tristan," I breathe, reaching to touch his face. "That's wonderful."

He captures my hand, his expression uncertain. "Is it? The King of Haldonia admitting he needs help? We've already given them enough to talk about with the baby announcement."

"It's not admitting weakness," I say firmly. "It's claiming your strength."

His eyes search mine in the darkness. "My father would have called it pathetic. Kings don't show vulnerability. They don't talk about their feelings. They certainly don't seek therapy."

"Your father was wrong about many things," I remind him gently. "And look where his approach led the country. Look what it did to you."

Tristan shifts, sitting up against the headboard. I move with him, unwilling to break our physical connection.

"What made you decide?" I ask, my anger softening at his vulnerability.

He's quiet for a long moment. "The nightmares are getting worse. Our fight tonight"—he looks away, ashamed—"when I stormed out, it was because I felt myself losing control. The pressure of everything... the aftermath of the war...it's been too much."

My heart aches for him. I take both his hands in mine. "All the more reason why this is the right decision. Especially with the baby coming."

He nods, his gaze drifting to my growing belly. The press conference announcing the pregnancy last week had been front-page news across Haldonia. The people's excitement for a royal baby had momentarily overshadowed the criticism Tristan had been facing over his decision to end the conflict with our neighboring country.

"I don't want to be that person," Tristan whispers. "I don't want our child to grow up with a father who can't control his anger, who walks out when things get hard."

"That's exactly why counseling is such a good idea," I tell him. "You're already taking steps to change. Breaking the cycle before our baby arrives."

His hand moves to rest on my stomach, where our child has just started to make its presence known with tiny flutters. "I felt terrified at the press conference, you know. Not about the public knowing, but about what kind of father I'll be."

He pulls me close, burying his face in my hair. "What if the country finds out? What if they see it as weakness? A king who needs therapy after ending a war…they're already watching our every move since the pregnancy announcement."

I pull back, framing his face with my hands. "Listen to me. You've already shown more strength than anyone who's ever worn this crown. Strength isn't about hiding your struggles—it's about facing them. About being brave enough to say, 'I need help' and then seeking it out."

"The parliament—"

"Can go to hell," I interrupt, surprising a laugh out of him. "Sorry, that wasn't very queenly of me."

"No, it was perfectly you," he says, his eyes warming. "And that's what I need. You, reminding me that I'm not just a king."

"You're going to be an amazing father," I tell him. "And an even better king because you're willing to do the work. To heal."

His hand strokes my rounded belly gently. "I still can't believe we're having a baby. Sometimes I worry that I don't deserve this happiness. Not after everything that happened in the war."

"The country already loves the idea of this child," I remind him. "New life, new beginnings. They stood and applauded at the press conference, remember?"

He shifts closer, his arms encircling me protectively. "I want to be better for them. For you. For our child. I never want to walk out on you again like I did tonight."

"You already are better," I whisper, leaning my forehead against his. "The fact that you're even having these thoughts proves it. You question yourself, and you want to improve—that's what makes you different."

"I don't know about that." A small smile plays at his lips. "I question almost every decision I make these days."

I laugh softly. "See? That's actually a good thing. Perfect certainty can be dangerous."

We sit in comfortable silence, his hand making gentle circles over the swell where our child grows. I can feel some of the tension from our argument leaving both of us.

"Shannon says the baby news has improved our approval ratings," I say, smiling a little.

"Of course she's tracking that." He shakes his head. "And about Dr. Merrick—"

"That's private," I assure him. "Between you and me and him. The country doesn't need to know everything, Tristan. Some things are just for us."

He nods, relief evident in his expression. "I start on Thursday."

"I'm proud of you," I tell him. "So proud."

"Even though I'm terrified?" His voice drops to a whisper. "Even though I walked out during our fight?"

"Especially because you're terrified and doing it anyway. And because you came back." I press my lips to his. "That's what real courage looks like."

He kisses me back, deep and slow, his hands tangling in my hair. When we part, the worry lines around his eyes have softened.

"Do you forgive me? For leaving like that?" he asks, vulnerability raw in his voice.

"I do," I say softly. "We're both learning, Tristan. Neither of us had perfect examples of how to do this."

"Another reason to be better than those who came before us," he says, a new determination in his voice.

I settle back against his chest, our argument fading into reconciliation. His arms wrap around me, one hand resting protectively over our growing child. For all the complexity of our lives, for all the weight of the crown we share, this moment feels like coming home.

"I love you," he murmurs into my hair.

"I love you too," I whisper back. "Both of you."

As I drift toward sleep, I feel a peace replacing the turmoil of the night. Tomorrow will bring its challenges—it always does. But tonight, in the darkness before dawn, with Tristan's heart beating steadily beneath my ear and our baby growing within me, I know that whatever comes, we'll face it together. The king, the queen, and the tiny heir on the way.

It's not the fairy tale I imagined as a girl, but it's better. It's real. And it's ours.

CHAPTER 12
TRISTAN

I sit in Dr. Merrick's waiting room, my leg bouncing with nervous energy. The magazines on the side table remain untouched. I'm not here to catch up on celebrity gossip or the latest political scandal. I'm here because I need to get my head straight before our baby arrives.

Five months. Just five more months until I'm a father. The thought both exhilarates and terrifies me.

"King Tristan?" Dr. Merrick's assistant appears at the doorway. "She's ready for you now."

I nod, rising to my feet. Parker shifts in his seat across the room, always vigilant. "I'll be right here, sir."

Dr. Merrick's office is deliberately calming—soft blue walls, comfortable furniture, and large windows that let in streams of natural light. She rises from behind her desk when I enter, extending her hand with a warm smile that never seems forced or performative.

"Your Majesty, thank you for coming," she says, gesturing toward the plush armchair across from hers. "I was able to rearrange my schedule when your office called. I understand this is your first session?"

"Thank you for fitting me in," I say, settling into the chair. The tension of exposing my vulnerabilities to a stranger sits heavy on my shoulders, but I'm desperate enough to try anything.

"Of course." She sits, crossing her legs and placing her notepad on her lap. "Perhaps we could start with what brings you here today?"

I exhale slowly, considering how to begin. "Nightmares. Flashbacks. Things I thought I'd buried deep enough."

She nods, her expression remaining neutral but attentive. I appreciate that—no shock, no pity, just professional focus.

"Can you tell me about these nightmares?" she asks.

"The village. The orders. The aftermath." My throat tightens as I speak. "I'm back in the valley, watching as my unit moves forward. I can hear the commander's voice in my ear, telling me we have to neutralize the threat, that intelligence confirms enemy combatants are hiding among civilians."

"And in the dream?" she prompts gently when I pause.

"In the dream, I see their faces before I give the order. In reality, they were just blurred shapes in the distance. But in the dream..." I swallow hard. "In the dream, one of them is always Amelia. And recently, she's been holding our baby."

Dr. Merrick makes a small note. "It sounds like these nightmares might be intensifying with your current circumstances. Major life changes often trigger stress responses, especially in those who have experienced trauma."

"Becoming a father is about as significant as it gets," I say with a humorless laugh.

"Are you afraid of fatherhood itself, or something specific related to it?"

The question hangs in the air, and I take my time answering it, wanting to be honest with her—and with myself.

"I'm afraid of losing my temper," I finally admit, the words feeling like stones in my mouth. "My father...he wasn't physically abusive, but his anger was legendary. Cold, calculated, devastating. He could cut you down with just his words and a look." I lean forward, resting my elbows on my knees. "What if I'm like him? What if the war broke something in me that can't be fixed? What if I'm holding our child and have a flashback? What if I—"

"Tristan," Dr. Merrick interrupts, using my name without title—surprising me with her directness. "You're catastrophizing. Let's back up and deal with what's actually happening, not with what might happen."

I take a deep breath, nodding. I didn't expect such frankness in a first session, but perhaps that's what I need.

"Have you told Amelia about these fears?"

"Not entirely. She knows about the nightmares, but not about my fear of turning into my father. Or worse."

Dr. Merrick sets her notepad aside. "Why not?"

"Because she's four months pregnant, and I don't want to burden her with my issues. She has enough to deal with."

"Do you think she'd see it as a burden? Or as her husband trusting her with his feelings?"

I don't have an answer for that.

"What happened in the valley was tragic," Dr. Merrick continues. "You were following orders in a combat situation with limited information. The fact that you still struggle with it shows your humanity, not your monstrosity."

"But what if—"

"Let me give you some practical tools for when you feel yourself slipping into those dark moments," she says, redirecting me. "First, I want you to concentrate on what we call grounding techniques," she explains, before continuing on. "When you feel yourself getting triggered, find five things you can see, four you can touch, three you can hear, two you can smell, and one you can taste."

I nod. Now that I know what it is, I've tried this before, and it does help sometimes.

"Second, I want you to create a physical reminder—something small you can carry with you that represents what you're fighting for. Not as a king, but as a man. Something that reminds you of Amelia and your child."

"Like what?"

"That's for you to decide. Some people carry a photo, others a small token with significance. Whatever feels right to you."

I think about it, already having an idea of what might work.

"Third, and perhaps most important, I want you to practice strategic retreats. When you feel your emotions becoming overwhelming, give yourself permission to step away briefly. Not to avoid the situation, but to regulate your response to it."

"You want me to walk away when I'm angry?" The idea feels counterintuitive.

"Not permanently. Just long enough to regain control. Tell whoever you're with—whether it's Amelia or eventually your child—that you need a moment and then return when you're calmer."

I consider this. "My father never walked away. He'd just keep going until you broke."

"And is that who you want to be?"

"No," I say firmly. "It's not."

We spend the rest of the session discussing more strategies—journaling, specific breathing exercises, scheduling regular time for physical activity to burn off excess stress. By the time we finish, I feel both exhausted and strangely lighter.

"Would you like to schedule a regular time moving forward?" Dr. Merrick asks as we stand.

"Yes, please." I pause, then add, "I appreciate your directness. It's refreshing."

She smiles. "That's what you're paying me for, Your Majesty. Not to coddle you, but to help you become the man you want to be."

As Parker drives me back to the palace, I stare out the window, thinking about everything Dr. Merrick and I discussed. The weight of responsibility—to my country, to Amelia, to our unborn child—sometimes feels crushing. But today, for the first time in weeks, it also feels manageable.

"Everything all right, sir?" Parker asks, meeting my eyes in the rearview mirror.

"Getting there," I reply.

When we arrive at the palace, I head straight to my office, needing a moment to process before seeing Amelia. I close the door behind me and walk to my desk, opening the bottom drawer where I keep personal items. Among them is a small wooden box that belonged to my grandfather—the king everyone says I take after, not my father.

Inside, I find what I'm looking for—my grandfather's compass. He gave it to me before his death, telling me it would always help me find my way home. As a child, I took it literally. Now, I understand the metaphor.

This could be the token Dr. Merrick suggested—a physical reminder of who I want to be, of the legacy I want to create.

I slip the compass into my pocket just as my phone rings. It's Kate, my new assistant. She's promised to keep me on track.

"Sir, I've moved your interviews to Thursday as requested. You're free to leave early on Friday."

"Thank you, Kate. That's perfect."

After we hang up, I sit there for a moment, thinking about Dr. Merrick's advice to be honest with Amelia. We need time away from the palace, away from the constant demands of the crown. We need space to talk, truly talk, before our child arrives.

With newfound determination, I leave my office and head to our private quarters. I find Amelia in our sitting room, a book open on her lap, one hand resting protectively over her growing belly. The sight of her still takes my breath away.

She looks up, her face brightening. "You're home earlier than I expected."

"I rearranged some things." I cross the room and sit beside her, taking her hand in mine. The compass in my pocket presses against my thigh, a comforting weight. "Lia, what do you think about going to the beach house this weekend? Just the two of us. We can leave early Friday."

Her smile widens, reaching her eyes in that way that makes my heart skip. "I would love to," she says, squeezing my hand. "More than anything."

CHAPTER 13
AMELIA

The next afternoon, I'm folding another sundress and tucking it into my suitcase, trying to ignore the dull ache in my lower back. The beach house waits for us—our sanctuary away from the palace, away from prying eyes and scheduled appearances. Just Tristan and me for three glorious days.

"You're bringing too many outfits," Shannon comments, perched on the edge of my bed. "It's only a weekend."

"Says the woman who isn't growing out of her clothes by the hour." I hold up a flowing maxi dress, examining it skeptically. "This fit last week. Now I'm not so sure."

Shannon laughs, but her eyes are gentle. "Your belly's barely showing, Amelia."

"Tell that to my waistbands." I toss the dress into the suitcase anyway. "And don't get me started on my bras. Who knew pregnancy would make everything hurt so much? My breasts feel like they've been used as punching bags."

"The price of creating royalty," Shannon quips, reaching for the dress I just packed and refolding it more neatly.

I collapse onto the bed next to my suitcase, dramatically throwing an arm over my eyes. "I've been sick every morning this week. The royal physician says it's normal, but there's nothing dignified about puking into priceless antique toilets."

"At least Tristan holds your hair back."

"True." I smile despite myself. "He's been annoyingly perfect about everything. Gets up with me no matter how early, makes sure there's crackers by the bed." I rub my still-flat stomach thoughtfully. "I think he's more excited than I am sometimes."

Shannon's quiet for a moment, her hands pausing over my suitcase. I lift my head to look at her.

"Everything okay?"

She smiles, tucking a strand of hair behind her ear. "I wanted to tell you...Parker and I are getting more serious."

I sit up immediately, my nausea forgotten. "Oh? Do tell."

"It's different now," she says, a blush creeping up her neck. "We've been dating for months, but lately it feels like we're moving to another level."

"I've noticed you two seem happier." I smile. "The way he looks at you when he thinks no one's watching."

"We've been talking about moving in together," Shannon admits, her voice dropping slightly despite us being alone.

"Shannon!" I grab her hands, delighted. "That's a big step."

"It just feels right." She shrugs, but can't hide her happiness. "Last night he told me he's never felt this way about anyone before."

"About time he admitted it." I grin. "Remember when you two tried to keep it professional at that state dinner and failed miserably?"

Shannon laughs. "We thought we were being so discreet."

"Please. Tristan and I knew the moment you walked in." I squeeze her hands. "I'm so happy for you both."

"It's strange," she says thoughtfully. "When we first started dating, I worried it would complicate work. But it's made everything better somehow."

She shakes her head, but she's still smiling. "It's been...nice. Different than I expected. He's not as uptight as he seems at work."

"I imagine not." I wiggle my eyebrows suggestively.

"Amelia!" She laughs, snatching a pillow and swatting me with it. "It's new. We're taking it slow."

"Sure you are." I dodge another pillow swing. "But slow enough that I should book separate rooms for you at the next diplomatic function, or…?"

Her blush deepens. "Maybe not that slow."

I fall back laughing, wincing as the motion makes my tender breasts ache again. "Ouch. Damn these hormones. Everything hurts, everything makes me cry, and everything about my husband makes me want to tear his clothes off."

"Poor you," Shannon says, utterly unsympathetic. "Forced to be attracted to your devastatingly handsome husband."

"You don't understand," I groan, reaching for my swimsuit and stuffing it into a side pocket. "Yesterday I watched him sign documents for thirty minutes and nearly jumped him on the council table. His fingers, Shannon. Just…holding a pen. I almost embarrassed the entire monarchy."

"Pregnancy hormones are no joke," she agrees, helping me zip the overflowing suitcase. "Parker mentioned that Tristan had to reschedule a meeting last week because you—"

"We don't need to discuss that," I cut her off quickly, heat flooding my face. "That was a private royal matter."

"Of course, Your Majesty." She gives a mock curtsy, smirking.

The bedroom door opens, and Tristan appears, already changed for our drive to the coast. My mouth goes dry at the sight of him in dark jeans and a blue button-down, sleeves rolled to just below his elbows.

"Ready, Lia?" he asks, and then notices my expression. "What?"

"Nothing," I say too quickly. Shannon snorts beside me.

He glances between us, suspicious. "Am I interrupting something?"

"Just girl talk," Shannon says, standing and straightening her skirt. "I was just telling Her Majesty that the car is packed and ready. You should reach the beach house before sunset if you leave now."

"Perfect." He crosses to the suitcase, lifting it effortlessly. "Feels like you packed for a month, not a weekend."

"Your child is demanding extra wardrobe options," I inform him primly, standing and smoothing my dress over my belly.

His eyes soften the way they always do when I mention the baby.

"My apologies to both of you then." He turns to Shannon. "Parker's finalizing the security detail. You two have everything covered here?"

"Of course." She nods. "The official statement is that you're reviewing coastal properties for potential development. No press, no appointments. Your phones will be diverted to us for anything that's not an actual emergency."

"You're the best," I tell her, pulling her into a quick hug. "And I want details about you and Parker when I get back."

"Amelia," she hisses, glancing at Tristan.

He holds up his hands. "I know nothing, and I wish to know nothing about my head of security's personal life."

"Liar," I call him out. "You were betting on them too."

Tristan gives Shannon an apologetic shrug. "For what it's worth, I thought he had more patience."

Shannon shakes her head, looking heavenward as if asking for strength. "You two deserve each other. Now go, before someone finds a reason to keep you here."

Ten minutes later, we're in Tristan's Range Rover, the one indulgence he allows himself that isn't strictly royal approved. The palace gates close behind us, and I feel the weight of the crown lifting with each mile marker we pass.

Tristan drives with one hand on the wheel, the other resting on my thigh. I watch the way his fingers flex as he navigates a curve, the tendons in his forearm shifting beneath tanned skin. My mouth goes dry.

"You're staring," he says, eyes still on the road.

"Can't help it." I trace a finger along his wrist where it emerges from his rolled sleeve. "Have I ever told you that you have the sexiest wrists I've ever seen?"

He laughs, glancing over at me. "That's a new one. Should I be concerned about these pregnancy hormones?"

"Absolutely." I shift in my seat, moving his hand slightly higher on my thigh. "I've been thinking about your hands all day. The way your fingers looked around your pen during that meeting this morning..." I trail off, biting my lip.

His grip tightens slightly on my leg. "If I recall correctly, we were nearly late to that meeting because of similar observations about my hands."

"Your fault for looking so good making coffee," I murmur, leaning over to press a kiss to his shoulder. "How much longer until we reach the beach house?"

His eyes remain fixed on the road, but I don't miss the way his jaw tightens. "Hour and a half, at least."

"Too long," I sigh dramatically, settling back in my seat.

"Patience, Lia." His thumb traces small circles on my thigh. "We have the whole weekend."

"Says the man who isn't experiencing the hormone equivalent of being seventeen again." I place my hand over his, guiding it higher. "Besides, you're the one always telling me how important it is to take advantage of our private moments."

Tristan shoots me a look that makes my pulse race. "If I pull over now, we'll never make it to the beach before dark."

"Would that be so terrible?" I ask innocently.

He laughs, shaking his head. "The things I do for my queen."

As he signals and begins looking for a suitable turnoff, I smile to myself. The crown may be heavy sometimes, but moments like these— just us, just Tristan and Amelia—these are the moments that make everything worthwhile.

Whatever challenges await us back at the palace can wait. For now, there's just the open road, the man I love, and three days of freedom stretching before us. And at this particular moment, those are the only royal duties I care about fulfilling.

CHAPTER 14
TRISTAN

The drive to the beach house is quiet, peaceful. Amelia dozes in the passenger seat, her hand resting protectively over the small swell of her belly. Five months pregnant, and somehow more beautiful every day. I glance at her while keeping my eyes mostly on the road, stealing these small moments to appreciate her without the weight of royal obligations pressing down on us.

Parker follows in the car behind, maintaining a respectful distance. He's given us this illusion of privacy, though I know he's vigilant, watching for any sign of the threat I still can't shake from my mind.

"We're almost there," I say softly as Lia stirs, her eyes fluttering open. She smiles that smile—the one that still makes my heart skip even after all this time.

"I must have fallen asleep," she mumbles, straightening in her seat. "Sorry for abandoning you on the drive."

"You needed it." I reach across to take her hand. "You're growing our child. Sleep all you want."

She laughs, the sound light and airy against the backdrop of the ocean coming into view. "If only the royal court could hear you now, encouraging your queen to be lazy."

"The royal court can kiss my—"

"Tristan!" she cuts me off with mock horror, but her eyes sparkle with amusement.

I grin, unrepentant. These moments—when we can just be us, without the weight of a nation on our shoulders—these are what I live for now.

The beach house comes into view, its weathered wood exterior standing in stark contrast to the polished marble of the palace. It's modest by royal standards, which is precisely why I love it.

This isn't just a cottage. It's freedom.

"This is heaven," Lia sighs, sinking into the corner of the oversized couch, her feet tucked under my thigh. Outside, rain has begun to fall, pattering against the windows in a soothing rhythm. The security team completed their sweep hours ago, and now it's just us—just Tristan and Amelia, not the king and queen.

"Better than the palace?" I ask, already knowing her answer.

"A thousand times better," she says, reaching for another handful of popcorn from the bowl balanced on my lap. "No advisers knocking every five minutes, no formal dinners, no itineraries…"

"No suits," I add, gesturing to my worn jeans and faded university sweatshirt.

"Definitely no suits, though you do look devastatingly handsome in them." She winks, and I feel a rush of warmth that has nothing to do with the fire crackling on the hearth.

The movie plays on, some romantic comedy she picked, but I'm hardly paying attention. Instead, I'm watching her—the way she laughs without restraint here, how her shoulders have lost the tension they carry in the palace, how her hair falls loose around her face instead of styled for public appearance.

"You're staring," she says without looking away from the screen.

"I'm admiring," I correct her. "There's a difference."

This pulls her attention from the movie. "Oh? And what exactly are you admiring, Your Majesty?"

I catch her hand, pulling it to my lips. "Everything. But mostly how you look when you're not being watched by the entire country."

Her expression softens. "And how do I look?"

"Free," I say simply. "Like the woman I fell in love with."

She sets the popcorn aside and shifts closer to me. "I am that woman. Always. Even when I'm playing the role of queen."

"I know." And I do. It's one of the countless reasons I love her—her ability to remain authentically herself despite the crushing expectations of royal life.

Her lips find mine, soft at first, then with increasing intensity. I taste salt from the popcorn and something uniquely Lia that I've never been able to define. My hands find her waist, drawing her closer still.

"The movie," I murmur against her mouth, though I couldn't care less about it.

"Will still be there later," she finishes, moving to straddle my lap, her belly a gentle pressure between us, a reminder of the miracle we've created together.

Her kisses become more urgent, and I match her passion, letting my hands roam beneath her oversized sweater, feeling the warmth of her skin. This is another kind of freedom—the freedom to touch my wife without concern for propriety or who might be watching.

"I love you," I breathe against her neck. "God, Lia, I love you so much it terrifies me sometimes."

She pulls back, framing my face with her hands. "Why does it terrify you?"

I hesitate, not wanting to darken the mood, but we've always been honest with each other. "Because I've never had anything this good in my life. Because I keep waiting for it to be taken away."

Her eyes hold mine, steady and sure. "I'm not going anywhere, Tristan. Neither is this baby. We're your family now, and nothing—not the crown, not anything—is going to change that."

I want to believe her with every fiber of my being. And when she's here, in my arms like this, I almost do.

She leans in to kiss me again when suddenly she gasps, her body going rigid.

"What?" Alarm shoots through me. "What's wrong? Is it the baby?"

But instead of pain, her face shows wonder. She grabs my hand, guiding it to the side of her belly. "Wait," she whispers. "Just wait."

For a moment, there's nothing. Then I feel it—a distinct tap against my palm, like a tiny knock from inside her.

"Oh my god," I whisper, awestruck. "Is that—"

"Yes." She laughs, tears springing to her eyes. "That's our baby."

The tap comes again, stronger this time, a definitive kick. Something shifts inside me, the plates of my heart realigning. Until now, the baby has been an idea, a future. But this—this is real. This is my child, making their presence known.

"Hello in there," I say softly, bending to speak directly to Lia's belly. "It's your dad." The word catches in my throat. Dad. I'm going to be someone's father. Someone worthy of this tiny person's trust.

As if in response, there's another kick, right against my hand. A laugh escapes me, part joy, part disbelief.

"I think they recognize your voice," Lia says, her fingers threading through my hair.

"You think so?" The idea fills me with a fierce pride.

"Definitely. You talk to them every night before bed. They know who you are."

I press my lips to the spot where I last felt movement. "I can't wait to meet you," I whisper. "We're going to be okay, the three of us. I promise."

Lia's hand finds mine, our fingers intertwining over the swell of our child. In this moment, I believe it. We will be okay. We have to be.

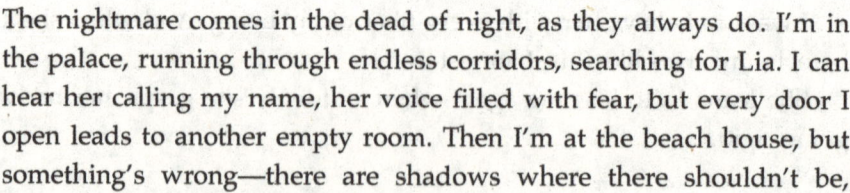

The nightmare comes in the dead of night, as they always do. I'm in the palace, running through endless corridors, searching for Lia. I can hear her calling my name, her voice filled with fear, but every door I open leads to another empty room. Then I'm at the beach house, but something's wrong—there are shadows where there shouldn't be, whispers in the dark corners. I find Lia in our bedroom, but when she turns, her face is blank, her eyes empty.

"You couldn't protect us," she says, her voice not her own. "Just like you couldn't protect the country."

I wake with a gasp, heart pounding against my ribs, sweat slicking my skin despite the cool night air coming through the open windows. Beside me, Lia sleeps peacefully, one hand splayed across her belly, her breathing deep and even.

Careful not to wake her, I slip out of bed and pad to the bathroom, splashing cold water on my face. The man in the mirror looks haunted, dark circles under his eyes no amount of royal advisers can erase.

"Get it together," I whisper to my reflection.

But the unease lingers, that sense of something watching, waiting. The same feeling I've had for weeks now, the one Parker insists is just royal paranoia.

I return to the bedroom, but instead of getting back into bed, I go to the dresser where I put my grandfather's old compass. It's nothing special to look at—brass, tarnished with age, the glass face slightly clouded—but it was his most treasured possession. "So you always know which direction to go," he'd told me when he placed it in my twelve-year-old hands.

I sit on the edge of the bed, running my thumb over the worn surface. My grandfather was the only one who understood the weight that awaited me. "Being a good king isn't about never bending," he'd said. "It's about knowing when to bend so you don't break."

The compass needle swings, finding north with unerring accuracy even after all these years. There's something comforting in its constancy, its certainty. No matter how lost I feel, north is still north.

I close my eyes, focusing on the solid weight of the compass in my palm, anchoring myself to the present. Lia is here. Our baby is here. They're safe. I'm safe.

"Tristan?" Lia's voice is thick with sleep. "What's wrong?"

I turn to find her watching me, propped up on one elbow, her hair a tousled halo around her face.

"Just a dream," I say, trying to keep my voice light. "Go back to sleep."

But she knows me too well. She sits up, reaching for my hand. "The same one?"

I nod, not trusting my voice.

She glances at the compass in my hand and understanding softens her features. "Come here," she says, tugging me back down beside her.

I stretch out, and she curls against me, her head on my chest, her belly pressed against my side. I keep the compass clutched in my free hand, its edges pressing into my palm.

"We're okay," she whispers, her breath warm against my skin. "We're right here."

"I know." And in this moment, with her weight solid against me and the compass as my anchor, I do know. Whatever threats may be out there—real or imagined—they can't touch this. They can't touch us.

I press a kiss to the top of her head, breathing in the scent of her hair. "Go back to sleep, love. I'm okay now."

She makes a soft sound of contentment, already drifting off. I stay awake a while longer, listening to her breathe, feeling the occasional flutter of movement from our child. The compass remains in my hand, a reminder that even in the darkest night, direction can be found.

Eventually, sleep reclaims me, and this time, no dreams come. Just darkness, warm and safe, with Lia's heartbeat as my lullaby.

CHAPTER 15
AMELIA

The scent of salt air mingles with coffee as I pad barefoot across the cool wooden floors of our beach house. Sunlight filters through the wide windows, catching dust motes that dance in the golden beams. This place has always felt different than the palace—simpler, more honest. Here, the weight of crowns and duty seems to lighten, if only for a few precious days.

I find Tristan in the kitchen, his back to me as he whisks eggs in a bowl. He's wearing faded jeans and a simple white T-shirt that stretches across his shoulders. It's a far cry from the tailored suits and formal attire that the world sees, and I treasure these moments when he's just mine.

"Good morning," I say, sliding my arms around his waist from behind.

He turns in my embrace, bowl still in hand. "I was going to surprise you with breakfast in bed."

"I couldn't stay asleep knowing you weren't there," I confess, rising on tiptoe to kiss him. He tastes like coffee and possibility.

"Well, now that you're up, you can help." He nods toward the counter where fresh bread, butter, and a bowl of berries await. "I thought we'd make French toast."

I reach for the bread, beginning to slice it. "My favorite."

"I know." His smile is soft, private—the one only I get to see.

We move around each other in the kitchen with practiced ease, a dance we've perfected over the months of our marriage. I dip the bread in the egg mixture while he heats the pan. Our hands brush as we work, small moments of connection that send sparks down my spine even after all this time.

I glance out the window and catch a glimpse of Parker standing on the edge of the property, pretending to survey the landscape while speaking into his phone. Even here, he maintains his vigil, though he's giving us the illusion of privacy.

"Parker's been on that call for twenty minutes," I say, nodding toward the window.

Tristan follows my gaze and sighs. "Something about the trade agreement with Norland. I told him we'd handle it Monday."

"Yet he's still here," I observe, pouring more coffee into our mugs.

"Keeping his distance, at least," Tristan says, sliding the golden-brown toast onto a plate. "Though he did mention it was, and I quote, 'of the utmost importance.'"

"Everything is 'of the utmost importance' to Parker," I say, rolling my eyes. "The man would consider a paper cut a national crisis."

Tristan laughs, the sound rumbling through his chest. "He takes his job seriously."

"Too seriously," I counter. "But I suppose that's why he's good at it."

"Just like Shannon is for you."

I nod, thinking of my own assistant. "She texted last night to remind me about the charity gala next weekend."

"As if we could forget," Tristan says, bringing our plates to the small kitchen table. We sit across from each other, the simplicity of the moment not lost on me. In the palace, we'd be dining in the formal breakfast room, attended by staff, our every move noted and cataloged for posterity. Here, we're just us.

I take a bite of the French toast, closing my eyes as the sweet, buttery flavor spreads across my tongue. "This is perfect."

"High praise from Queen Amelia," he teases, reaching across to wipe a smudge of syrup from my lip with his thumb.

"Just Lia here," I remind him. "Just yours."

His eyes darken at my words, that familiar intensity making my heart skip. "Always mine."

We finish breakfast talking about nothing important—a book I'm reading, a film he wants to see, the neighbors down the beach who've been renovating their house for what seems like eternity. Normal conversations. Precious in their ordinariness.

After we clean up, Tristan suggests a walk on the beach. The air is still crisp, hovering between winter and spring, but the sun promises warmth later. I bundle up in one of Tristan's sweaters, the sleeves falling past my fingertips, and slip on a pair of boots.

"Ready?" he asks, holding out his hand.

I lace my fingers through his. "Ready."

The beach is nearly empty this early in the morning, just a few dedicated joggers and people walking their dogs. The tide is retreating, leaving behind a wet canvas of sand that reflects the clouds above like a mirror. We walk in companionable silence for a while, our footprints marking our path behind us.

"I've been thinking," Tristan says finally, his voice almost lost in the rhythm of the waves.

"A dangerous pastime," I quip, squeezing his hand.

He chuckles. "I've been thinking about us. About how different things could have been."

I look up at him, studying the profile that's become so familiar to me. The strong jaw, the slight crook in his nose from a childhood injury, the fan of dark lashes. "Different how?"

"If we hadn't been who we are. If I hadn't been born the crown prince, if you hadn't been—"

"The sacrificial lamb?" I offer with a wry smile.

He winces. "I was going to say, 'the daughter of a diplomat.'"

"Semantics." I shrug, but there's no bitterness in my tone. Not anymore.

We stop walking, and Tristan turns to face me, taking both my hands in his. The wind whips my hair around my face, and he tucks a strand behind my ear with gentle fingers.

"Do you ever regret it?" he asks, his eyes searching mine. "The arrangement. The way we started."

I consider my answer carefully. There was a time, in the early days, when I might have said yes. When the weight of expectation and duty felt like chains around my throat. But now…

"No," I say honestly. "I don't regret it. Not anymore."

Relief softens his features. "No?"

I shake my head, looking past him to the house perched on the dunes behind us. Our sanctuary. Our escape. "This place changed everything for me," I admit.

His brow furrows. "What do you mean?"

I take a deep breath, the salt air filling my lungs. "During the war, when you sent me here for safety—" I pause, the memories still raw despite the months that have passed. The uprising. The violence. The fear that gripped our small nation while rebels attempted to overthrow the monarchy.

Tristan's hands tighten around mine. "You don't have to talk about it."

"I want to," I insist. "I need to."

He nods, giving me space to find the words.

"When I was here, alone with just the security detail, I was afraid I'd never be able to look at this house the same way again." The confession tumbles out of me. "I thought it would feel like a prison, a reminder of the worst time in our lives, of how close we came to losing everything."

Tristan's eyes are stormy with emotion. "Lia—"

"But it doesn't," I continue, needing him to understand. "Instead, it's become my safety. Our safety. I love it here because when I look at these walls, I don't see the fear anymore. I see the place where I realized how much I truly loved you. How terrified I was of losing you."

His expression softens, vulnerability etched across his features. "You never told me this before."

"It wasn't something I could put into words until now," I explain, shivering slightly as a gust of wind cuts through the sweater. "When you were fighting to keep the peace in the capital, when the reports kept coming in about the violence, all I could think was 'Please, let him come back to me.' And that's when I knew."

"Knew what?" he asks, his voice husky.

"That what started as an arrangement had become so much more. That somewhere along the way, the man I was obligated to marry had become the only man I could imagine spending my life with." I look up at him, blinking back tears. "I realized I wasn't trapped in a political marriage. I was desperately in love with my husband."

Tristan pulls me to him, wrapping his arms around me as if he could shield me from the memories, from the cold, from anything that might hurt me. I feel the rapid beat of his heart against my cheek.

"I thought I'd lost you that day," he murmurs into my hair. "When the palace was breached, before I knew you'd made it safely here…"

I press closer to him, remembering the frantic phone call, his voice tight with fear as he ordered me to evacuate. "But you didn't. We're here. We survived."

"We did more than survive," he says, pulling back just enough to look into my eyes. "We won. Against the rebels, against the odds, against anyone who said our marriage was just a political move."

I smile up at him, my heart full. "We did."

He kisses me then, deeply and thoroughly, his lips warm despite the chill in the air. I melt into him, my body recognizing its other half, my soul finding its home.

When we part, breathless and flushed, I see the desire in his eyes that mirrors my own. "Race you back to the house?" I challenge, already pulling away.

Tristan laughs, the sound carried away by the wind. "What do I get if I win?"

I throw a mischievous look over my shoulder as I start to run. "Me!"

I hear his footsteps in the sand behind me, gaining ground quickly with his longer stride. I don't mind losing this particular race. In fact, I'm counting on it.

The beach house grows larger as we approach, no longer a symbol of confinement or fear, but of liberation. Of love. Of the truth that sometimes, the things we're bound to by duty become the very things that set us free.

And as Tristan catches me at the bottom of the wooden steps, lifting me into his arms with a triumphant grin, I know with absolute certainty that I am exactly where I'm meant to be.

CHAPTER 16
TRISTAN

The waves crash against the shore in a steady, soothing rhythm that I've come to associate with peace. Sitting here on the deck of our beach house, Lia's head resting on my shoulder as we watch the sun begin its descent toward the horizon, I feel a contentment I never thought possible.

"What are you thinking about?" she asks, her voice soft against the backdrop of the ocean.

I run my fingers through her hair, savoring the silky texture. "How lucky I am," I answer honestly. "How different everything is now."

She shifts to look up at me, those eyes that caught me from the first moment we met still having the same effect on me now. "Good different?"

"The best different," I assure her, dropping a kiss on her forehead. "I never imagined I could have this."

Her hand finds mine, fingers intertwining as naturally as breathing. The slight swell of her belly presses against my side, our child growing stronger each day within her. Sometimes I wake in the middle of the night just to place my hand there, to feel the connection to this new life we've created.

"Have you thought any more about the nursery?" Lia asks, following my gaze to where my free hand rests on her stomach.

"I was thinking maybe a sky theme," I suggest. "Stars and clouds on the ceiling. Something timeless."

She smiles, that radiant expression that makes my heart stumble every time. "I like that. Not too gendered, calm, peaceful."

"Exactly." I nod, picturing it in my mind. "The painters could start next week if we approve the design when we get back."

The sun touches the water now, setting the ocean ablaze with orange and gold fire. Our last evening here before returning to the reality of royal duties tomorrow. These stolen moments at the beach house have become our sanctuary, the place where we can just be Tristan and Amelia, not King and Queen.

"We should probably talk about the nanny situation," I say, reluctant to break the spell but knowing these practical matters need attention. "Kate sent over the files of the final candidates yesterday."

Lia sighs, snuggling closer. "I know it's necessary, but part of me wishes we could do it all ourselves."

"Me too." I kiss the top of her head, inhaling the familiar scent of her shampoo. "But with our schedules...I want to be there for every moment I can, but—"

"But you're the king," she finishes for me. "And I have my duties too."

"We'll make it work," I promise. "The right nanny will be an extension of us, not a replacement. And we'll carve out sacred family time that nothing can interrupt."

She nods against my chest. "I liked the woman from Finland. The one with the background in early childhood development."

"Ingrid," I recall. "She seemed kind. Experienced too."

"And she didn't seem intimidated by the whole royal thing," Lia adds with a small laugh.

"That's definitely a point in her favor." I smile, remembering how the woman had regarded us with respectful professionalism rather than the awkward deference that makes both of us uncomfortable.

The sun is halfway below the horizon now, painting the sky in deepening shades of purple and crimson. I'll never tire of this view, especially with Lia beside me.

"I've made a decision," I say after a moment of comfortable silence. "I'm going to continue with therapy."

She turns to look at me, surprise and something else—pride, maybe —in her expression. "You are?"

"Yes." I take a deep breath, still finding it difficult to articulate these things even with her. "Dr. Merrick has been helping me understand… everything I went through and how it affected me emotionally."

Lia places her palm against my cheek, her touch grounding me. "I think that's a wonderful idea, Tristan."

"You do?" Something in me still expects criticism for this choice, still hears my father's voice dismissing therapy as weakness.

"Of course I do." Her voice is firm, leaving no room for doubt. "Healing isn't weakness. It's one of the bravest things you can do."

I turn to kiss her palm, overwhelmed with gratitude for this woman who sees me—truly sees me—and loves me anyway. "I want to be better," I whisper. "For you. For our child. For Haldonia."

"You already are." Her eyes shine with unshed tears. "But I'm proud of you for doing this."

We fall silent again, watching as the last sliver of sun disappears beneath the waves, leaving behind a canvas of stars beginning to emerge in the darkening sky. The beach house has become our refuge, but the castle is our home—complicated as it may be with all the responsibilities it represents.

"We should probably start packing," Lia says eventually, though neither of us moves to get up.

"Five more minutes," I bargain, pulling her closer.

She laughs softly. "You said that twenty minutes ago."

"Time moves differently here," I insist with a grin. "Royal decree."

"Oh, is that how it works?" She raises an eyebrow, the teasing light in her eyes making me want to kiss her.

So, I do, capturing her lips with mine, slow and sweet and full of promise. She responds immediately, her hand coming up to curl around the nape of my neck, holding me to her as though I'd ever want to pull away.

When we finally part, both a little breathless, I rest my forehead against hers. "I love you, Lia. More than I ever thought possible."

"I love you too," she whispers back, the simple words carrying the weight of everything between us.

Eventually, we do make our way inside to pack for the return journey tomorrow. Parker has already arranged the security detail, and Kate has managed to clear my schedule for the morning, so we don't have to rush. These small mercies make the transition back to royal life a little easier.

Later, as we lie in bed, the sound of the ocean a constant companion through the open windows, Lia traces patterns on my chest with her fingertips.

"Are you nervous?" she asks. "About going back?"

I consider the question seriously. "Not nervous exactly. But I'm always aware of the weight of it all when we return. Here, I can almost pretend we're just a normal couple expecting a baby. There..." I trail off, not needing to explain further.

"There, you're the king who's changing everything," she finishes. "The reformer who's shaking up centuries of tradition."

"And you're the commoner queen who stole the heart of a nation," I add with a smile, running my hand along the curve of her hip.

She laughs. "Is that what they're calling me now?"

"Among other things. All good, I promise. The people adore you, Lia. Even more than they tolerate me."

"They don't tolerate you," she corrects gently. "They're beginning to trust you. There's a difference."

I hope she's right. The path I've chosen isn't the easy one, pushing for reforms that my father would have considered sacrilege. But it's the right one, I'm certain of that.

"Get some sleep," Lia murmurs, pressing a kiss to my chest. "Tomorrow will be busy."

She falls asleep quickly, her breathing evening out into a rhythm as familiar to me now as my own heartbeat. I lie awake a little longer, watching the moonlight play across her features, committing this peaceful moment to memory to carry with me into whatever challenges await us at home.

The drive back to the capital takes longer than expected, a sudden summer storm forcing the Range Rover to slow to a crawl for safety. Parker, ever vigilant, sits in the front passenger seat, occasionally checking in with others who are watching CCTV via an earpiece.

"Everything all right?" I ask after the third such exchange.

He turns slightly. "Yes, sir. Just standard protocol with the weather conditions."

I nod, trusting him implicitly as always. Beside me, Lia dozes lightly, the pregnancy making her tired more easily these days. I keep my arm around her, letting her use my shoulder as a pillow despite the formal suit I'm already wearing in preparation for our return.

As we finally approach the city limits, Parker's posture changes subtly. "Sir, there appears to be a gathering near the castle approach."

Instantly alert, I feel my body tense. "What kind of gathering?"

"Not a security concern," he assures me quickly. "Civilians. Quite a number of them."

My mind races through possibilities—a protest? Some news while we were away? "Do we know what it's about?"

"Reports indicate they're supporters, sir." There's something almost like amusement in Parker's usually stoic expression. "Many are holding signs."

This wakes Lia, who blinks sleepily. "What's happening?"

"Apparently we have a welcoming committee," I tell her, squeezing her hand reassuringly.

As our car turns onto the main avenue leading to the castle gates, I see them—hundreds of people lining both sides of the street, umbrellas open against the light rain that still falls. And Parker was right—they're holding signs.

"HALDONIA STANDS WITH KING TRISTAN"

"REFORM NOW"

"LONG LIVE THE QUEEN"

"THANK YOU FOR FIGHTING FOR US ALL"

Lia's hand tightens in mine as she takes in the scene. "Oh, Tristan," she breathes.

For once, I'm speechless. These aren't the wealthy elite who have traditionally surrounded the monarchy. These are ordinary Haldonians —shopkeepers, teachers, factory workers, students—standing in the rain to show their support.

"Should I slow down, sir?" our driver asks.

I hesitate only briefly. "Yes. And lower the windows, please."

Parker gives me a sharp look but doesn't object when I add, "Just a crack. Enough to acknowledge them."

As the windows lower, the sound of cheering reaches us, growing louder as people realize we can hear them. I raise my hand in acknowledgment, and the cheers intensify.

"They believe in you," Lia says, her voice thick with emotion. "They believe in what you're trying to do."

The lump in my throat makes it hard to respond. All these months of fighting against the old guard, pushing for changes that would give more Haldonians a voice, a chance at better lives—there have been times I've questioned whether it was worth the constant battle. Whether I was fooling myself that one person, even a king, could really make a difference.

But looking at these faces, these ordinary citizens willing to stand in the rain to show their support, I know with certainty that we're on the right path.

"We have to keep going," I say, as much to myself as to Lia. "No matter how hard it gets."

She takes my hand and places it on her stomach, where our child grows stronger each day. "For the future," she says simply.

"For the future," I agree, as our car continues slowly down the avenue toward home, surrounded by the people who remind me why every struggle is worthwhile.

I may never be the king my father wanted me to be. But looking at these faces, hearing their voices raised in support, I think perhaps I'm becoming the king Haldonia needs. And with Lia by my side, and our child on the way, I've never been more determined to honor their faith in me.

The castle looms ahead, still imposing with its centuries of history, but no longer feeling like a prison. Instead, it's becoming what it should always have been—the heart of a nation moving forward together. And as we pass through the gates, I carry the image of those rain-soaked supporters with me, a reminder that we're not alone in this fight.

Not anymore.

CHAPTER 17
AMELIA

Monday morning arrives with a vengeance. My alarm blares at five thirty a.m., and I silence it before it can wake Tristan. He came to bed late after a call with the ambassador from neighboring Bellovia. I slip out from under the covers, careful not to disturb him, and make my way to the bathroom.

The mirror reflects a paler version of myself than I'm comfortable with. I splash cold water on my face, willing the color to return to my cheeks. "This pregnancy glow they talk about is a myth," I whisper to my reflection, placing my hand on my round stomach.

By seven, I'm dressed and reviewing my schedule with Shannon in my office.

"The children from St. Mary's Academy will be arriving at nine for the library dedication," she says, sliding a folder across my desk. "Your speech is inside, along with background on the school. The press will be there."

I nod, skimming the speech. "Have we confirmed the hospital visit for Wednesday?"

"Yes, though the Minister of Health suggested postponing until after flu season. He's concerned about exposure in your condition."

"I won't postpone. Those children have been waiting for this visit."

I push the folder back toward her, suddenly feeling a wave of dizziness wash over me.

Shannon notices immediately. "Amelia? Are you all right?"

I take a deep breath, steadying myself. "Fine. Just the usual pregnancy stuff." I place a hand protectively over my abdomen. "Let's go over the rest of the week."

The morning proceeds as planned. The library dedication goes smoothly, though the flash of cameras and the scent of fresh paint make my stomach churn. I manage to make it through my speech, focusing on the excited faces of the children rather than the growing discomfort in my abdomen.

By noon, I'm back in my office, attempting to focus on correspondence when the nausea hits with unexpected force. I barely make it to the private bathroom, emptying what little breakfast I managed to eat into the toilet. Cold sweat breaks out across my forehead as I grip the porcelain, willing my stomach to settle.

A gentle knock sounds at the door. "Amelia?" Shannon's voice is tinged with concern.

"Just a minute," I call back, my voice weaker than I intended. I rinse my mouth and check my appearance in the mirror. The woman staring back looks ghostly.

When I emerge, Shannon's eyes widen. "That's it. I'm calling Dr. Bennett."

"No," I protest, but the room tilts suddenly, and I grasp the doorframe to keep from falling. "It's just morning sickness. It'll pass."

Shannon guides me to the sofa. "Morning sickness doesn't usually include that shade of green. Not to mention you haven't had a ton of it the entire time you've been pregnant. Please, let me call him."

Before I can argue further, another wave of nausea sends me rushing back to the bathroom. This time, there's nothing left to bring up, but my body doesn't seem to care. I retch painfully as Shannon holds my hair back.

"This isn't normal," she says firmly. "Even for pregnancy."

I slump against the wall, too exhausted to argue.

"The entire kingdom is invested in this baby, Amelia. We can't take chances." She dampens a cloth and presses it to my forehead. "The king asked me to keep an eye on you while you were working. He's worried."

Another wave of nausea crashes over me, and this time, when it passes, I nod weakly. "Call Dr. Bennett."

Shannon doesn't waste time. Within twenty minutes, the royal physician is in my office, his face grave as he examines me.

"Your Majesty, how long have you been feeling like this?" he asks, taking my blood pressure.

"The nausea started with my pregnancy, but it was mild. Today it's...different." I close my eyes against the light that suddenly seems too harsh.

"Any other symptoms? Fever? Headache?"

I nod slightly. "Both. Since this morning."

Dr. Bennett exchanges a look with Shannon. "I'd like to run some tests. This doesn't appear to be typical morning sickness."

Fear grips me—fear for the tiny life growing inside me. "The baby?"

"Let's not jump to conclusions," he says gently. "But I would feel more comfortable if you came to the hospital where we have better facilities."

I want to protest, to insist that I just need rest, but the room won't stop spinning. "Call Tristan," I whisper to Shannon.

The next few hours blur together. I'm vaguely aware of being helped into a car, of Shannon making quiet phone calls, of the hospital's sterile hallways. Blood is drawn, monitors attached, questions asked that I struggle to answer through the fog in my mind.

"Virus," I hear Dr. Bennett say at some point. "Not uncommon but concerning given her condition."

"And the baby?" Tristan's voice cuts through my haze. When did he arrive?

"Stable for now, but we need to get Her Majesty's fever down and keep her hydrated."

I force my eyes open to find Tristan sitting beside my bed, his face etched with worry. He looks disheveled, his tie loosened and hair mussed, as if he's been running his hands through it repeatedly.

"Hey," I manage, reaching for his hand.

Relief washes over his features. "You scared the hell out of me, Lia."

"I'm sorry," I murmur.

"Don't apologize." He brings my hand to his lips, kissing it gently. "Dr. Bennett says you have some kind of virus. They want to keep you overnight for observation."

Panic flutters in my chest. "But the meeting with the education board is tomorrow—"

"Canceled," he says firmly. "Everything's canceled. You and our heir are the only things that matter right now."

A nurse enters, hanging a new IV bag. "This should help with the dehydration, Your Majesty. The doctor has ordered something for the nausea as well."

I nod gratefully, already feeling the cool rush of fluids entering my system. When she leaves, Tristan moves from the chair to sit carefully on the edge of my bed.

"Parker had to physically restrain me from leaving the summit when Shannon called," he admits, his thumb tracing circles on my palm. "I've never left a meeting that fast in my life."

Despite everything, I smile. "What will the ambassadors think?"

"I don't give a damn what they think." His voice is low, intense. "When I heard you were in the hospital..." He trails off, swallowing hard.

I squeeze his hand. "I'm going to be fine. We both are."

Tristan's eyes drop to my stomach, and he places his palm gently over it. "You're sure?"

"Dr. Bennett seems confident. It's just a virus. Bad timing, but nothing that won't pass."

He exhales shakily. "I should have been there. I knew you weren't feeling well when we left the beach house."

"Stop," I say, more firmly than I've been able to speak all day. "This isn't your fault. Besides, you can't cancel the kingdom every time I feel a little under the weather."

A small smile tugs at his lips. "Watch me."

"The public will start to worry if they hear I'm hospitalized," I say, thinking of the headlines that are likely already circulating.

"Let them worry. Parker's already handling the press. Just a standard statement about the queen resting under doctor's supervision. Nothing about the virus or risk to the baby."

The medication begins to work its way through my system, dulling the nausea and making my eyelids heavy. Tristan notices immediately.

"Sleep," he urges, brushing hair from my forehead. "I'll be right here."

"You should go back to the palace," I murmur, fighting to stay awake. "There's that call with the prime minister..."

He shakes his head. "Parker's handling it. I'm not leaving you."

As I drift toward sleep, I feel Tristan shift to stretch out beside me on the narrow hospital bed, careful not to disturb the IV or monitors. His arm creates a protective barrier around me, his warmth a comfort against the chill of the room.

"I love you," he whispers against my hair. "Both of you."

In this moment, despite the sterile surroundings and the lingering discomfort, I feel profoundly safe. Tomorrow will bring its own challenges—rescheduled appointments, concerned staff, and the inevitable press frenzy over the health of Haldonia's future heir. But tonight, in the circle of Tristan's arms, I allow myself to simply be Amelia—not the queen, not the public figure, just a woman loved fiercely by her husband.

"We love you too," I whisper back, and let sleep claim me at last.

CHAPTER 18
TRISTAN

The steady beep of the heart monitor has become my companion through the night. I've counted each pulse, matching them to my own heartbeats, finding comfort in their rhythmic certainty while everything else feels so precarious.

I shift in the bed and check my watch. 4:17 a.m. The fluorescent lights in the hallway cast an unnatural glow under the door, making sleep nearly impossible, though that's not what's kept me awake. It's the sight of Amelia, my Lia, lying in the hospital bed next to me, her face pale but peaceful in sleep, one hand resting protectively over her stomach.

Our baby. The thought still catches me off guard sometimes, flooding me with equal parts terror and joy.

When the nurse pushes the door open, I turn so that I can see her, fully alert. She gives me a sympathetic smile as she checks Lia's vitals.

"How is she?" I whisper, not wanting to wake my wife.

"Improving steadily," the nurse says, making notes on her tablet. "Blood pressure's back to normal. That's very good." She glances at me, taking in my rumpled suit and the dark circles under my eyes. I got rid of my jacket at some point, but I'm not exactly comfortable. "You should try to get some real sleep, Your Majesty."

I shake my head. "I'm fine right here."

She doesn't argue, having learned over the past twenty-four hours that the King of Haldonia isn't leaving his wife's side, royal duties be damned.

When the door closes behind her, I roll over, and press the heels of my hands against my eyes. The image of Lia collapsing yesterday during the library dedication is burned into my memory—her face suddenly draining of color, her hand reaching for me as her knees buckled. I've never moved so fast in my life, catching her before she hit the floor, the room erupting in gasps and shouts. I've watched the video that someone recorded more times than I care to admit. It's as if I'm punishing myself because I wasn't there.

"You're thinking too loud."

My head rolls over at the sound of Lia's voice, rough with sleep but the most beautiful sound I've heard in hours. Since the last time I heard her talk, all I've wanted is to hear more words, to know she's okay.

"Hey," I say, turning back over, taking her hand in mine. "How are you feeling?"

She smiles weakly. "Like I've been run over by the royal carriage." Her free hand moves to her stomach. "Is the baby—"

"Fine," I say quickly, placing my hand over hers. "The baby's fine. Just perfect. The doctor said it was just dehydration and exhaustion brought on by the virus. Your body telling you to slow down." I don't mention that we already discussed most of this. I know she's worried.

The relief in her eyes makes my chest tighten. "I was so scared," she whispers.

"Me too." I bring her hand to my lips, pressing a kiss to her knuckles. "But you're both okay, and that's all that matters."

"What time is it?" She glances toward the window, where the first hints of dawn are starting to appear.

"Too early. Go back to sleep."

She studies my face, her eyes softening. "Have you slept at all?"

I shrug. "Here and there."

"Liar," she says, but there's affection in her voice.

"Lia, I don't think—"

"Since when does the King of Haldonia worry about hospital proto-col?" She opens her arms up to me. "I'll sleep better with your arms around me."

It's all the invitation I need. I carefully pull her to me, mindful of the IV in her arm, and she nestles against me with a contented sigh. I press a kiss to her temple, breathing in the scent of her hair, and for the first time since she collapsed, I feel the knot of fear in my chest begin to loosen.

"Parker will have a fit if he finds us like this," I murmur against her hair.

She laughs softly. "Let him. Even he wouldn't dare separate us."

I finally drift off to the steady rhythm of her breathing, waking only when the nurses come to check on her, holding my breath each time until they confirm that everything is still stable.

Morning brings Dr. Bennett, who reviews Lia's chart with an approving nod. "Your blood pressure is back to normal, and all your other labs look good, Your Majesty," she tells Lia. "I think we can discharge you today, provided you follow my instructions about rest."

"She will," I say before Lia can respond. "I'll personally see to it."

Dr. Bennett smiles, turning to me. "I'm sure you will, Your Majesty. I want her on bed rest for the next three days, limited activity for the week after that, and then we'll reassess. She needs to stay hydrated, keep her stress levels low, and rest." He gives Lia a pointed look. "That means delegating some of your charitable work, ma'am."

Lia opens her mouth to protest, but I squeeze her hand. "We'll make it happen," I promise.

Two hours later, after signing discharge papers and navigating through the hospital with Parker creating a security bubble around us, we're in the car heading back to the palace. Lia leans against me, looking exhausted just from the short journey from her room to the car.

"Kate called while you were getting dressed," I tell her, my arm around her shoulders. "She's rescheduled all my appointments for the next three days."

Lia looks up at me, surprised. "Tristan, you don't have to—"

"Yes, I do." My tone leaves no room for argument. "The country can survive without me for a few days. You and our child are what matter most to me."

"But the education reform bill—"

"Will still be there next week." I press my lips to her forehead. "Nothing is more important than you. Nothing."

She relaxes against me, too tired to argue further, and I silently thank whatever gods might be listening that she's not fighting me on this. The thought of returning to meetings and royal duties while she recovers alone is unbearable.

At the palace, I carry her from the car to our private apartments despite her protests that she can walk. Parker follows discreetly behind, his eyes constantly scanning for threats, though he says nothing about my breach of royal protocol. Even he knows better than to get between me and Lia right now.

Shannon meets us at the door to our suite, her face lined with worry. "Your Majesties, I've had the staff prepare—"

"Thank you, Shannon," I cut her off gently. "Can you please ensure we're not disturbed for the rest of the day unless it's an emergency? And have some light food sent up in about an hour?"

"Of course, sir." She steps aside, allowing me to carry Lia into our bedroom.

Once I've settled Lia in our bed, propped up against pillows, I sit beside her, taking her hands in mine. "What do you need? Anything at all?"

She smiles softly, reaching up to touch my face. "Just you. You look exhausted, Tristan."

"I'm fine." I catch her hand, pressing a kiss to her palm. "I need to make a statement to the public. They've been worried about you."

"You haven't made one yet?"

I shake my head. "Parker's been handling the press. I wanted to wait until I had good news to share." I don't tell her about the hours I spent pacing in the hospital corridor, praying to a God I'm not sure I believe in, making bargains with the universe to keep her and our baby safe.

"Go," she says, squeezing my hand. "Make your statement and then come back to me. I'm not going anywhere."

I hesitate, reluctant to leave her side even for a moment.

"I promise I'll still be right here," she adds with a knowing smile. "Go be king for ten minutes, then come back to being just my husband."

With a sigh, I stand, straightening my jacket. "Ten minutes," I agree, leaning down to kiss her. "Not a second more."

In my office, Parker and Kate wait with the communications team. They've drafted a statement, but I barely glance at it before handing it back.

"I'll speak from the heart," I tell them, adjusting my tie as the camera is set up. "No script."

Kate raises an eyebrow but doesn't argue. She's learned when to push and when to let me have my way.

When the red light on the camera blinks on, I take a deep breath, thinking of Lia upstairs in our bed, safe and recovering.

"People of Haldonia," I begin, looking directly into the camera. "As many of you know, Queen Amelia was taken to the hospital yesterday after falling ill. I want to personally thank you for your prayers and well wishes during this anxious time."

I pause, allowing myself a small smile. "I am relieved and grateful to inform you that Her Majesty is now recovering at home. Both she and our unborn child are doing well, though the queen will be taking time to rest and recover over the coming days."

My voice softens slightly. "Becoming parents is the greatest joy and responsibility that Queen Amelia and I have ever faced. It is a journey we share with many of you, and one that reminds me daily of what is truly important—family, health, and the future we are building together."

I straighten, my resolve clear. "For the next few days, I will be stepping back from public duties to care for my wife. I trust you understand that my first duty must be to her, just as many of you would do for those you love."

"The business of government continues, of course. My staff and the Royal Council will address any urgent matters, and I will return to my full duties once the queen is fully recovered. We are both deeply touched by your concern and support during this time."

I nod once, signaling the end of the broadcast. The moment the camera light goes off, I'm already heading for the door.

"Sir," Parker calls after me. "The ambassador from—"

"Can wait," I finish for him, not breaking stride. "I meant what I said. For the next few days, I'm not king. I'm just a man taking care of his wife."

Back in our bedroom, I find Lia dozing against the pillows, one hand still resting protectively over her stomach. I quietly remove my jacket and tie, kick off my shoes, and slide into bed beside her, careful not to wake her.

She stirs anyway, eyes fluttering open. "How did it go?"

"Fine," I murmur, pulling her gently against me. "I told them the truth—that nothing is more important to me than you and our baby."

She smiles sleepily, nestling closer. "Not even Haldonia?"

"Not even Haldonia," I confirm, placing my hand over hers on her stomach. "The country will survive without me for a few days. But I wouldn't survive without you."

"That's treason, Your Majesty," she teases softly.

"Then arrest me." I press my lips to her forehead. "I'm guilty as charged."

As she drifts back to sleep in my arms, I think about what Parker said to me days ago, about not showing how much she means to me. He was wrong. My strength doesn't come from appearing invulnerable. It comes from knowing exactly what I'm fighting for.

And what I'm fighting for is right here in my arms.

CHAPTER 19
AMELIA

The sunlight slants through the windows, casting a warm glow across our bedroom. I roll over, my hand automatically reaching for Tristan, but his side of the bed is empty. A wave of nausea hits me, and I groan, pulling the covers over my head. This virus has been relentless, made worse by my pregnancy.

"Lia?" Tristan's voice comes from the doorway. "Are you awake?"

I peek out from beneath the duvet. "Unfortunately."

He strides across the room, a tray balanced carefully in his hands. The smell of tea wafts toward me, and for once, it doesn't make my stomach lurch. He sets the tray on the nightstand and sits beside me, his weight dipping the mattress.

"Shannon cleared your schedule for the next three days," he says, brushing hair from my forehead. "And I've postponed the summit with the Belgian delegates."

"You didn't have to do that," I protest weakly, though relief floods through me. The thought of sitting through diplomatic meetings while fighting the urge to vomit was not appealing.

"I absolutely did." His voice is firm but gentle. "Dr. Bennett said you need rest, and for once, I'm going to ensure you follow doctor's orders."

I push myself up against the pillows, wincing at the dull ache in my lower back. "What about the press? They'll notice if both of us disappear." Although he's told me he'll be unavailable. It still worries me.

"Parker's handling it. A mild case of exhaustion for the queen. Nothing concerning, just requiring a few days of rest." His fingers trace circles on the back of my hand. "The country can survive without us micromanaging it for seventy-two hours."

The fact that he's here, that he's rearranged everything to take care of me, makes my heart swell. Seven months into our marriage, and he still finds ways to surprise me.

"What's all this?" I gesture to the tray.

"Ginger tea with honey. Plain toast. And—" he reveals a small plate of saltine crackers with a flourish "—Dr. Bennett's recommendation for keeping the nausea at bay."

I take the tea, sipping it carefully. The warmth soothes my throat, and the ginger settles my stomach almost immediately. "You're too good to me."

"I'm exactly as good to you as you deserve." He kicks off his shoes and stretches out beside me, arm curling around my shoulders. "Now, I was thinking we could start with that show you've been wanting to watch. The one about the chef."

"You hate cooking shows," I remind him, nestling against his chest.

"I hate seeing you miserable more." He reaches for the remote. "Besides, I might learn something. God knows the palace chefs could use some competition."

I laugh, then immediately regret it as my stomach protests. Tristan notices my discomfort and pulls me closer, his hand resting protectively over my round stomach. The gesture is so tender, so intimate, that tears prick my eyes.

"Hey," he says softly, noticing the wetness on my cheeks. "What's wrong?"

"Nothing," I whisper. "Just…pregnancy hormones."

He doesn't look convinced, but he doesn't push. Instead, he turns on the television and finds the show. We settle into comfortable silence, broken only by my occasional commentary on the contestants' techniques and Tristan's good-natured complaints about the judges' expectations.

By midday, I'm feeling well enough to take a shower. Tristan insists on joining me, claiming he's concerned I might faint. It's a flimsy excuse, but I don't call him on it. Not when his hands are so gentle as they massage shampoo into my scalp, not when his lips press tender kisses to my shoulders.

"Better?" he asks as he wraps me in a plush towel.

"Much." I lean into him, inhaling the clean scent of his skin. "Though I could use a nap."

He carries me back to bed despite my protests that I can walk perfectly well and tucks me in as though I'm made of glass. It should be annoying—I've never been one for coddling—but there's something deeply comforting about letting him take care of me. About not having to be Queen Amelia for a few precious days.

I drift off with his hand stroking my damp hair, and when I wake, the room is bathed in the golden light of late afternoon. Tristan is seated by the window, reading through papers, his brow furrowed in concentration.

"I thought you were taking time off too," I call, my voice husky with sleep.

He looks up, his face softening. "Just reviewing a few documents. Parker dropped them off an hour ago."

"Come back to bed." I hold out my hand to him. "The documents can wait."

He doesn't need to be asked twice. Within seconds, he's beside me, his warmth enveloping me as he pulls me against his chest. His lips find mine in a kiss that starts gentle but quickly deepens. My body responds to his touch as it always does, a slow heat building within me.

"Tristan you might get sick," I breathe against his mouth. "We can't..."

"I know," he murmurs, his hands slipping under my nightgown. "But there are other ways I can make you feel good, and I don't give a fuck about myself. You should know that by now. I survived a war."

And there are. His fingers and lips work magic on my sensitive skin, drawing gasps and moans from my throat. He's attentive to every response, every shiver, every whispered plea. When I finally come apart under his touch, it's with his name on my lips and his steady gaze holding mine.

After, as we lie tangled together, his hand rests gently on my stomach.

"I can't believe there's a baby in there," he says, his voice soft with wonder. "Our baby."

The thought sends a thrill through me, a mixture of joy and nervous anticipation. "And this virus is certainly not making it any easier," I admit with a small laugh. "At least Dr. Bennett assured me it won't affect the baby."

He's quiet for a moment, his expression tender. "I'm just glad you're getting the rest you need," he says. "For both of you."

I place my hand over his. "You're going to be an amazing father."

"How can you be so sure?" There's vulnerability in his question, a rare glimpse of the insecurities that plague him.

"Because I know you," I say simply. "I see how you lead with compassion. How you put the needs of others before your own. How you've been caring for me these past two days." I turn to face him, cupping his cheek. "You're nothing like your father, Tristan. You never will be."

His eyes close briefly, as though my words have lifted a weight from him. "I love you, Lia. Both of you."

"We love you too." The words feel right, natural, even though our baby is still so tiny inside me.

We spend the rest of the day in lazy contentment, dozing and watching television, ordering food from the palace kitchen when hunger strikes. It's a rare bubble of normalcy in our decidedly abnormal lives, and I cherish every moment.

As night falls, Tristan draws a bath for me, adding lavender oil that fills the bathroom with its soothing scent. He sits behind me in the large tub, his chest a solid wall of warmth against my back, his hands massaging the tension from my shoulders.

"Thank you," I say, letting my head fall back against him. "For taking care of me. For putting everything on hold."

"You don't need to thank me for that." His voice rumbles through me. "It's what any husband would do."

"But you're not just any husband," I remind him. "You're the king. You have responsibilities—"

"None more important than you and our child." His tone leaves no room for argument. "The kingdom has survived centuries of monarchs with far less dedication than either of us have. It can manage for a few days."

I turn in his arms, water sloshing over the edge of the tub. "I can't wait to see you as a father," I confess. "To see you teach our child about history and politics and fishing at the beach house."

His smile is soft, almost shy. "I can't wait to see you as a mother. To watch you sing lullabies and read bedtime stories. To see your eyes in our daughter's face."

"Or your stubbornness in our son's," I tease.

"God help us if that's the case." He laughs, then grows serious. "We're going to change things, Lia. For our child, for all children in Haldonia. We're going to build a better country than the one we have now."

In that moment, looking at the determination in his eyes, I believe him completely. Whatever challenges await us—as monarchs, as parents—we'll face them together. And we'll win.

"I know we will," I whisper, sealing the promise with a kiss.

CHAPTER 20
TRISTAN

The pen slides from my fingers, clattering onto the desk as I rub my tired eyes. Three hours of policy review has my brain feeling like mush, but at least I've knocked out most of Kate's checklist. The silence in my office is broken by a soft knock at the door.

"Come in," I call, straightening up and expecting Parker or one of my advisers.

Instead, it's Lia who steps through the doorway, and my exhaustion evaporates at the sight of her. She's dressed more casually than usual in a loose sweater that drapes over her slightly rounded stomach and comfortable slacks. The pallor that's haunted her skin for the past week has faded somewhat, though dark circles remain under her eyes.

"Hey you," she says, her voice stronger than it's been since she caught that damn virus.

I'm on my feet in an instant, crossing to her. "Should you be up? Dr. Bennett said—"

"Dr. Bennett said I could move around as long as I don't overdo it," she interrupts, her hand finding mine. "And I was going crazy staring at our bedroom ceiling."

She feels fragile under my hands as I guide her to the couch by the window. The sunlight catches in her hair, turning the brown strands to honey and copper. "You scared me this time, you know that?"

"I scared myself." Her hand drifts to her stomach, a gesture that's become automatic these past few weeks. "But the baby's fine. That's what matters."

I place my hand over hers. Beneath our palms, our child grows, oblivious to the fear that seized me three nights ago when Lia's fever spiked dangerously high. "You both matter. Equally and immensely."

She leans her head against my shoulder, and I breathe in the scent of her—the lavender of her shampoo mingling with something uniquely Lia. "Shannon told me about the school visit today. I want to be there."

"Absolutely not," I say immediately, my protective instincts flaring. "You're supposed to be resting."

"I've been resting for three days straight," she counters, that familiar stubborn set to her jaw appearing. "I'm not asking to run a marathon, Tristan. Just to sit and meet some children."

I study her face, knowing that look all too well. She's already made up her mind. "The doctor said—"

"The doctor said limited activity is fine, and that's what this is." She reaches up, her fingers cool against my cheek. "Please. It would mean a lot to me."

I close my eyes, leaning into her touch. This is what Parker warned me about—my inability to deny her anything. But then again, he hasn't felt the crushing weight of fear I did watching her battle this illness, made worse by the pregnancy neither of us had anticipated so soon.

"One hour," I concede finally. "And you stay seated the entire time. And Parker stations someone with medical training nearby."

Her smile, the first genuine one I've seen in days, makes my chest tighten. "Deal."

"And you promise to tell me if you start feeling tired or unwell."

"I promise." She seals it with a kiss, soft and brief.

I help her settle more comfortably on the couch, retrieving the throw blanket from its back and draping it over her legs despite her eye roll. "I have a few more things to finish before they arrive. Rest here until then?"

She nods, already reaching for one of the books that permanently live on my side table. I return to my desk, sneaking glances at her every few minutes as if she might disappear if I don't. Her color is better today, and has been improving every day since she got home from the hospital. Now that we're four days out, we're all feeling better. She's been fever free for the last four days and desperately wants to meet with the kids like she promised. Still, the memory of her burning skin beneath my hands, of her labored breathing as I held her, haunts me.

An hour later, there's another knock at the door, and Parker's head appears. "Sir, the children from St. Agnes Primary will be arriving in the East Drawing Room in fifteen minutes."

"Thank you, Parker." I turn to Lia, who's already setting aside her book. "Ready?"

Her smile is answer enough. I help her to her feet, offering my arm for support that she accepts with minimal protest. Progress.

Parker raises an eyebrow at us as we exit the office. "Your Majesty, are you certain this is wise?"

"I'm certain that my wife is as stubborn as she is beautiful," I reply, earning a gentle elbow to my ribs from said wife. "Have someone from medical standing by, please."

"Already arranged, sir."

The East Drawing Room has been transformed for our young visitors. The antique furniture has been rearranged, creating an open space with cushions on the floor. Historical artifacts from the palace collection—the ones sturdy enough to withstand curious hands—are displayed on low tables with simple explanations beside them.

I settle Lia in a comfortable armchair positioned to give her a view of the entire room. "Remember, one hour."

"Yes, Your Majesty," she says with exaggerated deference, her eyes sparkling with mischief.

Before I can respond, the doors open, and the controlled chaos that is twenty-five eight-year-olds enters the room. Their teacher, a no-nonsense woman in her fifties, keeps them in a semblance of order as Shannon introduces us.

"Children, I present His Majesty King Tristan and Her Majesty Queen Amelia."

Twenty-five pairs of wide eyes stare at us. One little girl in the front gasps audibly, tugging at her friend's sleeve and whispering something that makes them both giggle.

I step forward, falling into the role I've practiced countless times. "Welcome to the Royal Palace. We're very glad to have you here today."

They respond with the rehearsed curtsy or bow their teacher has clearly drilled into them, though several wobble precariously in the process. One boy at the back remains frozen, mouth agape.

"Before we look at some of the palace treasures, does anyone have any questions for His Majesty?" Shannon asks.

Hands shoot into the air. Shannon points to a freckled boy near the front.

"Do you have a sword?" he asks, bouncing on his toes.

I laugh. "Several actually, though I don't use them much these days. They're mainly for ceremonies."

A little girl with braids is next. "Is that your real wife?" she asks, pointing at Lia.

"Yes, that's Queen Amelia," I answer, unable to keep the pride from my voice.

"She's pretty," the girl declares matter-of-factly.

"I think so too," I agree, catching Lia's eye and the blush spreading across her cheeks.

The questions continue—do I wear my crown to bed (no), do I eat cake every day (I wish), can I put people in the dungeon (absolutely not, and we don't have dungeons anymore). Throughout it all, I'm acutely aware of Lia watching, her smile growing as the children's enthusiasm builds.

When Shannon guides them toward the historical displays, I make my way back to Lia's side. "How are you holding up?"

"I'm fine," she assures me, though I don't miss the way her hand trembles slightly against the armrest. "They're wonderful."

Before I can suggest she take a break, the teacher approaches us, a shy little girl with glasses half-hidden behind her skirt.

"Your Majesties, Emma has a question she'd very much like to ask the queen, if Her Majesty is feeling up to it."

Lia straightens immediately, her entire demeanor softening as she focuses on the child. "Of course. What would you like to know, Emma?"

The girl peeks out, her voice barely above a whisper. "Is it true you're going to have a baby?"

The room doesn't quite fall silent, but several nearby children pause in their explorations, clearly interested in the answer. Our pregnancy is public knowledge, but these children probably don't know that, so Lia will probably play along.

Lia handles it with perfect grace. "Yes, Emma, it's true. But it's a bit of a secret right now, so we'd appreciate if you'd help us keep it quiet for a little while longer."

Emma nods solemnly, clearly thrilled to be entrusted with royal confidences. "My mom says you'll be a good mom because you're kind. Like the old queen was."

I watch Lia's face carefully, knowing how deeply she feels the weight of comparison to my mother, whose charitable works and gentle manner made her beloved throughout the country. My mother, who spent more time with sick children in hospitals than at state dinners. My mother, whose absence still aches like a phantom limb some days.

"That's very kind of your mom to say," Lia replies, her voice steady though I can see the emotion behind her eyes. "Queen Eleanor was an extraordinary woman. I can only hope to be half as good with children as she was."

"Can I..." Emma hesitates, then rushes forward. "Can I touch your hand? My mom says I should ask."

"Of course you may." Lia extends her hand, and Emma places her small fingers against Lia's palm with reverent care.

Something shifts in the room then. Perhaps it's the way Lia leans forward, her full attention on this one child as if she's the most important person in the world. Or maybe it's how naturally she draws Emma into conversation, asking about her school and her favorite subjects.

Whatever the catalyst, within minutes, Lia is surrounded by children. They approach cautiously at first, then with growing confidence as she welcomes each one with genuine interest. She listens to their stories with the same attentiveness she gives to prime ministers and diplomats. When a little boy proudly shows her his missing tooth, she reacts with appropriate awe.

I take a step back, content to watch from the periphery. This is Lia in her element—the woman I fell in love with showing through the royal facade we both maintain in public. The woman who became my queen through an arranged marriage, but who captured my heart so completely, I sometimes forget our beginning was orchestrated by others.

"She's a natural," Shannon murmurs, appearing at my elbow. "Just like your mother was."

"Better," I say quietly, watching as Lia helps a little girl fashion a paper crown from supplies the creative teacher must have brought along. "My mother was born into this world. Lia adapted to it beautifully."

Fell in love with me, I think but don't say. Even now, after everything we've been through in our marriage, the transformation of our arranged union into something so deep and genuine sometimes strikes me with the force of revelation.

I glance at my watch, realizing we've already exceeded the hour I'd promised Dr. Bennett. But Lia shows no signs of flagging. If anything, she seems energized by the children's presence, her earlier pallor replaced by a healthy flush.

One of the boys tugs at my sleeve, pulling me from my thoughts. "King Tristan, sir? Do you want to see the dragon I drew?"

I crouch down to his level. "I absolutely do."

For the next half hour, I find myself fully immersed in the children's world, admiring drawings, answering earnest questions, and even joining in when they decide to build a "castle" from cushions. Through it all, I keep Lia in my peripheral vision, monitoring her for any signs of fatigue.

When the teacher finally announces it's time to leave, there's a chorus of disappointed groans. Lia has ended up seated on a cushion on the floor, surrounded by a circle of attentive faces as she tells them a story I recognize—one from the book of folklore my mother used to read to me.

"Perhaps we can visit again someday," she promises as they reluctantly gather their things.

As the children file out, many of them offering careful bows and curtsies in farewell, Emma hangs back, approaching Lia one last time.

"Your baby is very lucky," she says with the certainty only children possess.

Lia's hand moves to her stomach, that protective gesture that makes my heart clench every time. "Thank you, Emma. I hope you're right."

When the room finally empties, leaving just the two of us with Parker standing discreetly by the door, I cross to where Lia still sits among the cushions.

"Time to get you back to bed," I say, extending my hands to help her up.

She allows me to pull her to her feet, swaying slightly as she stands. Only then do I see the exhaustion she's been hiding. "Worth it," she says, correctly reading my concerned expression.

"They adored you," I tell her, wrapping an arm around her waist to steady her. "Every single one of them."

"They were wonderful children." Her head drops to my shoulder as we walk slowly toward the door. "Your mother would have loved them."

"She would have loved you," I reply honestly, the words catching slightly in my throat. "She would have been so proud of the queen you've become."

Lia looks up at me, her eyes bright with unshed tears. "Do you really think so?"

"I know so," I assure her, pressing a kiss to her temple. "And so does Emma's mother, apparently."

We make our way back to our quarters, Lia leaning more heavily against me with each step. By the time we reach our bedroom, she's nearly asleep on her feet. I help her change into her nightclothes and settle her into bed, pulling the covers up around her.

"Stay," she murmurs, catching my hand as I turn to leave. "Just for a bit."

I stretch out beside her, careful not to jostle the mattress too much. "Better?"

"Much." She tugs my hand to rest over her stomach. "We're both better with you here."

I press my face into her hair, breathing in the scent of her, feeling the steady beat of her heart against mine. In this moment, the weight of the crown, the endless meetings and decisions, the constant scrutiny—all of it fades to background noise.

"I saw you today," she says sleepily. "With that little boy and his dragon drawing. You'll be an amazing father."

The words wash over me, soothing an anxiety I hadn't fully acknowledged. "We'll figure it out together," I promise, both to her and to myself. "Just like everything else."

Her breathing deepens as sleep claims her, but I remain where I am, keeping watch. Outside this room waits a kingdom that demands my attention. Policies to review, decisions to make, appearances to schedule. But for now, my world narrows to this bed, to the woman sleeping beside me, to the curve beneath my palm where our future grows.

In this moment, I am not a king. I am simply a man, holding what matters most.

CHAPTER 21
AMELIA

The morning light filters through the gauzy curtains of our bedroom, casting gentle shadows across Tristan's sleeping form. I study him for a moment, the peaceful rise and fall of his chest, the way his dark hair falls across his forehead. Even after these months of marriage, I still find myself in awe that this man—this king—is mine. I love that he's sleeping soundly now. The PTSD seems to have abated, at least for now.

I slip out of bed quietly, not wanting to disturb him, my hand instinctively cradling the rounded swell of my belly. At four months pregnant, there's no hiding the royal heir growing inside me. Today marks my official return to royal duties after being sidelined by that wretched virus for nearly two weeks. While the time in bed wasn't entirely unpleasant—Tristan made certain of that, checking on me between meetings, bringing me soup and tea himself despite the palace staff's protests—I'm eager to resume my responsibilities. The doctor assured us that the virus posed no risk to the baby, but Tristan had still been adamant about my rest.

The hot shower eases the last remnants of stiffness from my body. As I towel off and begin my morning routine, I catch my reflection in the mirror. My complexion has finally returned to normal, the pallor replaced by a healthy glow. I turn sideways, studying my profile and the unmistakable curve of my stomach under my robe. The palace tailors have been working overtime adjusting my wardrobe to accommodate my changing body.

"You're up early." Tristan's voice, rough with sleep, comes from the doorway. He leans against the frame, wearing only sleep pants that hang low on his hips.

"First day back," I explain, reaching for my moisturizer. "I want to be prepared."

He crosses the room in three strides, wrapping his arms around me from behind, his hands coming to rest on the swell of my belly. "You're sure you're ready? No one would fault you for taking another day."

I meet his concerned gaze in the mirror. "I'm ready. Besides, the charity gala won't plan itself."

His eyes drop to where his hands cradle our growing child. "You're the most beautiful woman I've ever seen," he murmurs, "and somehow even more breathtaking carrying our child." The reverence in his voice makes my heart swell.

His lips find my neck, and a shiver runs through me. "If you say so."

"Just promise you'll tell me if it becomes too much."

"I promise," I whisper, tilting my head to give him better access. His hands slide across the silk of my robe, and I briefly consider calling Shannon to tell her I'll be late.

As if reading my thoughts, Tristan steps back with a wicked grin. "Later," he promises, his eyes dark with intent. "We both have obligations this morning."

I pout playfully. "Being responsible is overrated."

His laugh follows me as I retreat to the closet to choose my outfit for the day.

"I'm thinking we set up auction tables along this wall," Shannon says, gesturing to the blueprint of the grand ballroom spread across my desk. "Silent auction items for the first hour, then we move to the live auction after dinner."

I nod, making a note on my tablet, shifting slightly in my chair to find a more comfortable position for my growing belly. "And what about entertainment? Has the symphony confirmed?"

"They have, and they're donating their time." Shannon tucks a strand of blonde hair behind her ear, checking her own notes. "Also, the chef has three menu options for your approval."

The familiar rhythm of work soothes me. Despite my illness, Shannon has kept everything running smoothly, and we're only slightly behind schedule for the Children of Heroes gala—our first major event focused on supporting children who lost parents during the war. It's a cause close to my heart, a way to honor those who sacrificed everything for Haldonia.

"You know," Shannon says, setting down her pen, "you could have taken another day or two. No one would have minded."

I shake my head. "I've been cooped up long enough. Besides, this gala matters." I tap the fundraising projections. "These children need more than just our sympathy."

"Your Majesty is very dedicated," she says with a smile that reaches her eyes. After working closely for months, Shannon has become more than just my secretary—she's become a friend, one of the few people in the palace who sees me as Amelia first, queen second.

"Speaking of dedication," I say, glancing at the clock, "did Parker confirm the reservation for tonight?"

"He did. Seven o'clock at Lumière. The owner is thrilled you've chosen his restaurant for your first public appearance since your illness." She smiles, adding, "He also mentioned they're preparing a special mocktail menu just for Your Majesty. The press is already buzzing about the royal couple's first night out since announcing the pregnancy."

I can't help but smile. The visit to the restaurant is Tristan's idea—a way to support local businesses while also letting the public see that their queen is recovered. The fact that Lumière is known for its romantic atmosphere and exceptional wine list is just a bonus.

"Perfect. Now, about these donor recognition levels…"

By late afternoon, I've reviewed budget projections, approved invitations, and selected auction items for the gala. My head is swimming with numbers and logistics, but there's satisfaction in the progress we've made.

"I think that's enough for today," Shannon declares, gathering her tablet and notes. "You don't want to overdo it on your first day back."

I stretch, feeling the tightness in my shoulders from hours hunched over paperwork. "You're probably right. Besides, I need to get ready for tonight."

"The blue Valentino?" she suggests. "It photographed beautifully at the embassy reception."

"Hmm, I was thinking the burgundy Ellie Saab maternity design. It's new, and Tristan hasn't seen it yet." I smile, already imagining his reaction. The designer had created several pieces specifically tailored to flatter my changing figure, embracing rather than hiding my pregnancy.

Shannon laughs. "Ah, so we're aiming to render His Majesty speechless in public."

"It's good for him," I say with a mischievous grin. "Keeps him on his toes. Besides, the public loves seeing the baby bump. Might as well give them a good view."

After Shannon leaves, I review one last document—a proposal for expanding the Children of Heroes program to include educational scholarships. It's ambitious, but with the right support, entirely achievable. I make a few notes before closing the file.

As I prepare to leave my office, there's a knock at the door. Parker enters, Tristan's ever-present shadow except when the king dismisses him—which happens frequently when we're alone.

"Your Majesty," he says with a slight bow. "His Majesty asked me to remind you about this evening and to say he's looking forward to it."

I smile. "Thank you, Parker. Please tell him I'm equally excited."

Parker hesitates, and I raise an eyebrow. "Something else?"

"He also asked me to give you this." He holds out a small velvet box.

My heart flutters as I take it. Inside is a delicate pair of ruby earrings that will match my dress perfectly. Trust Tristan to know exactly what I've chosen to wear without being told.

The note inside simply reads:

For my queen, who outshines every jewel. - T

❖ • ❖

"You're staring," I murmur, applying a final touch of lipstick.

Tristan, already dressed in a perfectly tailored suit, makes no attempt to deny it. "How could I not? You're breathtaking."

The burgundy dress drapes elegantly over my rounded belly before flowing gracefully to the floor, its empire waist and strategic design both highlighting and celebrating my pregnancy. The deep color makes my skin glow, and the slit up one side offers tantalizing glimpses of leg with each step. The ruby earrings catch the light when I move.

"My goddess," he whispers, approaching me slowly. His hand reaches out to caress the curve of my stomach with a tenderness that makes my breath catch. "Carrying my child, ruling at my side...I've never seen anything more beautiful in my life."

"The earrings are beautiful," I say, turning to face him, emotion thick in my throat. "Thank you."

He crosses to me, his hands settling on my waist. "They pale in comparison, but I'm glad you like them." His eyes darken as he takes me in. "Though now I'm reconsidering our public appearance. I'd much rather keep you all to myself tonight."

I laugh, placing my hands on his chest. "Duty calls, Your Majesty. Besides..." I lean closer, my lips nearly brushing his. "Anticipation makes everything sweeter."

His grip tightens. "You're playing with fire, Lia."

"Good thing I'm not afraid of getting burned." I press a kiss to the corner of his mouth, careful not to leave a lipstick mark. "Now, shall we?"

Lumière glows with warm light, its windows offering glimpses of crystal chandeliers and white tablecloths. As our car approaches, I can see the crowd gathered outside—a mix of paparazzi and curious onlookers hoping to catch a glimpse of their monarchs and, more specifically, the queen's growing baby bump.

"Ready?" Tristan asks, squeezing my hand. His other hand rests protectively over mine on my belly.

I take a deep breath and nod. "Ready."

The moment we step out of the car, camera flashes explode around us. Tristan's arm slides protectively around my waist as we navigate the short walk to the entrance. I smile and wave, projecting confidence and warmth despite the intrusive lenses. I can hear exclamations about the baby bump, and I instinctively place my free hand over my stomach in what has become a familiar gesture.

"Your Majesties," the owner greets us at the door with a deep bow. "It is the greatest honor to welcome you and the future heir to Lumière."

"The honor is ours," Tristan replies smoothly, his hand still possessively at my waist. "We've heard wonderful things about your restaurant."

Inside, the other diners rise as we enter, offering respectful bows and curtsies. I note with approval that while our security team is present, they're discreet, allowing the restaurant to maintain its intimate atmosphere.

We're led to a table in a semi-private alcove—visible enough to be seen by other patrons but positioned to allow some conversation without being overheard. It's a delicate balance, being public figures while trying to have something resembling a normal evening out.

"You're doing wonderfully," Tristan says quietly as we take our seats. "How are you feeling?"

"Good," I assure him, genuinely meaning it. "It feels right to be back."

The sommelier approaches with a bottle of the restaurant's signature wine for Tristan and a specially crafted non-alcoholic beverage for me, served in an equally elegant glass. As he pours, I notice the flashes of cameras through the windows—the paparazzi are still hovering, capturing every moment.

"To your health," Tristan says, raising his glass once we're alone. "To having you back at my side, where you belong, and to our little prince or princess." His eyes drop to my rounded stomach with such love that I feel tears prick at my eyes.

I clink my glass against his. "I wasn't aware I ever left."

His smile is private, intimate. "Being in the same palace isn't the same as having us both be fully present. I missed you, Lia, and I'm aware I was the one who wasn't emotionally present."

The sincerity in his voice warms me more than the room we're in. "I missed you too."

Throughout dinner—a magnificent seven-course affair showcasing local ingredients—Tristan finds reasons to touch me. His hand covers mine on the table. His fingers brush my bare shoulder when he leans in to speak. His thumb traces the inside of my wrist as the dessert is served.

Each touch is proper enough for public viewing but charged with meaning only I understand. By the time we finish our meal, I'm practically vibrating with need.

When a small orchestra in the corner begins playing, Tristan stands and holds out his hand. "Dance with me?"

The other diners watch as he leads me to the small dance floor. His hand settles on the small of my back, while the other rests gently on the curve of my belly, drawing me as close as my pregnant form allows as we begin to move to the music. The cameras outside go wild at this intimate display, the king publicly cherishing both his queen and unborn child.

"You know this will be on every front page tomorrow," I say, nodding subtly toward the windows where camera lenses are pressed against the glass.

"Good," he says, his voice a low rumble that travels down my spine. "Let them see how a king worships his queen."

His hold tightens, and I melt against him, following his lead as we move across the floor. In this moment, the crown feels lighter, the responsibilities less daunting. We are simply a man and a woman in love, dancing in a beautiful restaurant.

"I don't tell you enough," he murmurs against my ear, "how proud I am of you. The work you're doing for those children—it matters, Lia." His hand caresses my belly gently. "And you'll be an incredible mother to our child. The way you fight for those who cannot fight for themselves—I see it in everything you do."

I pull back slightly to look into his eyes. "It's what any decent person would do."

"No." He shakes his head. "It's what you do. You see needs others ignore and refuse to look away. It's one of the countless reasons I love you." His hand spans protectively over our growing child. "Both of you."

My heart swells, and I don't care about the cameras anymore. I reach up to touch his face. "Take me home, Tristan."

His eyes darken. "We should stay a bit longer. Make it worth their while," he gestures subtly to the other patrons, who are watching us with undisguised fascination.

"Then kiss me," I challenge. "Give them something to really talk about."

A slow smile spreads across his face. "As my queen commands."

When his lips meet mine, the restaurant fades away. There is only Tristan—his taste, his scent, his strength surrounding me. I don't hear the murmurs of approval from the other diners or the frantic clicking of cameras outside. I am entirely his, and he is mine.

When we finally part, his expression is tender and fierce all at once. "Let's go home," he says, his voice rough. "The rest of tonight belongs to us alone."

As we leave the restaurant, his arm firmly around my waist, I lean into his strength. The paparazzi calls our names, begging for one more photo, one more moment. One particularly bold photographer shouts, "Your Majesty, a hand on the royal bump!" Tristan doesn't even hesitate—he turns me gently toward him, placing both hands on my rounded belly in a possessive, protective gesture, his eyes never leaving mine. The cameras go wild, capturing the intimate moment between king, queen, and unborn heir.

Then he guides me steadily to our waiting car, his focus entirely on me.

Tomorrow will bring more work, more responsibilities, more challenges as we navigate our roles as monarchs. The charity gala will demand attention to a thousand details. The children who lost parents in the war need advocates and support. And in a few months, our lives will transform again with the arrival of our child.

But tonight—tonight is ours. And as the car pulls away from the curb, Tristan's hand finds mine in the darkness before coming to rest on my belly, his thumb tracing gentle patterns across the taut skin where our baby grows. In this moment, I am not just Queen Amelia of Haldonia.

I am simply Lia, loved completely by the man beside me, carrying the physical manifestation of that love beneath my heart. And that is the greatest privilege of all.

CHAPTER 22
TRISTAN

The door to our private quarters closes behind us with a satisfying click. I loosen my tie, watching as Lia slips off her heels with a sigh of relief that makes me smile. Tonight was good for us—a rare evening out, just the two of us, away from the constant scrutiny of royal duties. Parker managed to keep the paparazzi at a respectable distance, and for once, I didn't mind their presence hovering at the periphery of our evening.

"God, my feet are killing me," Lia groans, padding across the plush carpet in her stockings. Her hands move to the small of her back, supporting the gentle curve of her belly where our child grows.

"You shouldn't have worn those torture devices," I say, shrugging off my jacket and draping it over a chair.

She throws me a look over her shoulder. "A queen has standards to maintain, even with a basketball under her dress."

"That's hardly a basketball." I laugh, crossing the room to her. My hands find her waist, sliding around to cradle her stomach. Five months along, and the swell of her pregnancy still takes my breath away. "More like a softball—maybe."

"You're not the one carrying it," she counters, but leans back against my chest, her body relaxing into mine.

I press my lips to the curve of her neck, breathing in the scent of her perfume. "You're right. And you're magnificent for doing so."

She turns in my arms, her fingers working at the buttons of my shirt. "Such flattery, Your Majesty. What are you after?"

"Can't a man appreciate his wife without ulterior motives?" I ask, even as my hands drift lower, tracing the line of her spine through the silky fabric of her dress.

"Not when that man has that look in his eyes." Her voice drops to a whisper, and I watch as her pupils dilate slightly.

I raise an eyebrow. "What look would that be?"

"The one that says you're thinking decidedly un-kingly thoughts."

I laugh, the sound rumbling in my chest. "Guilty as charged."

Her fingers finish with my buttons, pushing the shirt from my shoulders. "Good thing I'm thinking decidedly un-queenly thoughts then."

I reach behind her, finding the zipper of her dress and slowly drawing it down. "Care to elaborate on these thoughts?"

The dress loosens, and she allows it to slip down her body, pooling at her feet in a whisper of expensive fabric. Standing before me in nothing but lace undergarments, her body changed by pregnancy in ways that make my heart race, she's never been more beautiful.

"I think," she says, stepping closer, her fingers tracing the waist-band of my trousers, "I'd rather show you."

I let her lead me to our bed, marveling at how this woman—my wife, my queen, the mother of my child—still affects me like this. Every touch of her skin against mine sends electricity coursing through my veins.

"Wait," I say, suddenly remembering. "Is this…are you comfortable with this? The doctor said—"

She silences me with a kiss. "The doctor said everything is perfectly normal and healthy. Unless you'd rather not?"

Her challenging smile is all the answer I need.

"I'd rather very much," I murmur against her lips.

We take our time, finding new ways to fit together around the curve of her belly. There's laughter when something doesn't quite work, whispered suggestions, and adjustments that lead to gasps of pleasure. It's different now, but no less passionate, no less meaningful. Perhaps even more so, knowing our child sleeps safely between us.

After, as we lie tangled in the sheets, her head on my chest and my hand stroking lazy patterns across her back, I feel a contentment that still surprises me. This quiet domesticity was never something I expected to cherish, yet here I am, treasuring these moments more than any state dinner or royal engagement.

"What are you thinking about?" Lia's voice is sleepy, her breath warm against my skin.

I press a kiss to the top of her head. "Just how lucky I am."

She makes a soft sound, somewhere between agreement and amusement. "We both are."

I don't tell her about the momentary flash of worry that crossed my mind—the constant, nagging fear that all of this happiness could be snatched away. Instead, I hold her closer and listen to her breathing slow as she drifts off to sleep.

"I'll protect you both," I whisper into the darkness. "Always."

❖

Sunlight streams through the gap in the curtains, pulling me from sleep. Lia is still curled against me, her body warm and soft. For a moment, I simply watch her sleep, the gentle rise and fall of her chest, the way her lashes cast shadows on her cheeks. Then I carefully extricate myself from her embrace, smiling as she mumbles something unintelligible and burrows deeper into the pillows.

I grab my phone from the nightstand and pad quietly to the sitting area of our chambers. Parker has already sent the morning briefing—security reports, weather, and the day's agenda. But it's the news notification that catches my eye. I open it to find pictures from last night splashed across the front page of the Haldonia Daily.

"ROYAL ROMANCE: KING TRISTAN AND QUEEN AMELIA ENJOY RARE NIGHT OUT."

The images are surprisingly tasteful—Lia and I entering the restaurant, her hand on my arm, the two of us leaving, my hand protectively at the small of her back, a candid moment caught through the window where we're both laughing, her head thrown back and my eyes fixed on her face with unmistakable adoration.

A year ago—hell, six months ago—these photos would have infuriated me. The intrusion into our private life, the constant lens focused on our every move. I would have called Parker, demanded to know how the photographers got so close, insisted on stricter measures for our next outing.

Instead, I find myself studying the images with something like gratitude.

"What's got you looking so serious this early?"

I glance up to find Lia watching me from the doorway, wrapped in her silk robe, hair tousled from sleep.

"The paparazzi were busy last night," I say, holding up my phone.

She crosses the room and curls up beside me, taking the phone to examine the photos. "Oh, these aren't bad at all. I actually look decent for once."

"You look stunning," I correct her, wrapping an arm around her shoulders. "You always do."

She turns to look at me, brow furrowed slightly. "You're not upset? Usually, these kinds of pictures put you in a mood for the entire morning."

I consider this, thinking about how to explain the shift I feel within myself. "I think I've realized something. These pictures...they're part of our story. Part of our child's history."

My hand drifts to her stomach, and she places hers over mine.

"Someday, our son or daughter will look at these and see how much we loved each other. They'll see that before they were born, we were just Tristan and Amelia, stealing moments together despite the crown."

Lia's eyes soften. "That's a beautiful way to look at it."

"I'm learning," I say, surprised by the truth of it. "The man I was before would have seen only the invasion of privacy. But now..." I pause, looking again at the images of us together. "Now I see the preservation of memories I might otherwise forget in the daily chaos of ruling."

She leans her head against my shoulder. "Your father would have a conniption if he heard you talking like this."

I laugh, the mention of my father no longer stinging as it once did. "All the more reason to embrace it then."

"Rebel," she teases.

"Only for the right causes," I reply, pressing a kiss to her temple.

We sit in comfortable silence for a moment, the palace waking up around us. Soon, we'll be swept into the machinery of royal obligations —meetings, appearances, decisions that affect millions. But for now, in this quiet morning light, we're just Tristan and Lia, expectant parents, marveling at how different life looks from the other side of love.

"We should frame one of these," Lia suggests suddenly. "The one where we're laughing. For the baby's room."

The thought of our child growing up with tangible evidence of our happiness before their arrival fills me with unexpected emotion.

"I'd like that," I manage, my voice rougher than I intended.

She looks up at me, her eyes knowing. "You're going to be an amazing father, Tristan."

"God, I hope so," I whisper, the weight of that responsibility settling on my shoulders alongside the crown. "I hope I can be everything this child needs."

"You will be," she says with such certainty that I almost believe her. "You're already everything I need."

I capture her lips with mine, pouring into the kiss all the words I can't quite form—my gratitude, my fear, my overwhelming love for her and the life we're building together.

When we part, she smiles that smile that still makes my heart stutter. "Now, Your Majesty, shall we face this day together?"

I stand, pulling her gently to her feet. "Together," I agree, and for the first time in a long while, I'm not afraid of what tomorrow might bring.

Because whatever comes, we'll face it side by side.

CHAPTER 23
AMELIA

The reflection staring back at me in the full-length mirror looks almost regal now. Six months into pregnancy, my body has transformed into something unfamiliar yet miraculous. My hands trace the pronounced curve of my belly, home to the future heir of Haldonia, while Shannon fusses with the hem of my emerald gown.

"You're glowing, Your Majesty," she says, standing to adjust the diamond pendant resting above my collarbone.

"It's the hormones," I reply with a smile. "Or the fact that I haven't had a glass of wine in months."

Shannon laughs, stepping back to assess her handiwork. The dress —custom-designed to accommodate my changing shape—cascades elegantly to the floor, the empire waistline accentuating rather than hiding my condition.

"The Children of Heroes gala is the most important event on your calendar this month," she reminds me, handing me a small clutch. "The press will be particularly invested in your appearance tonight."

"Because nothing says 'support war orphans' like obsessing over what a pregnant queen is wearing," I quip, but without malice. I've grown accustomed to the scrutiny, the constant evaluation of my appropriateness for the role that fate—and my heart—thrust upon me.

The door opens, and I don't need to turn to know it's Tristan. I feel his presence before I see him, that magnetic pull that's been there since the beginning.

"My God," he breathes, and our eyes meet in the mirror.

I turn, allowing him to take in the full effect. His formal military dress uniform accentuates his broad shoulders, medals reflecting the soft lighting of our chambers. He looks every inch the king he was born to be.

"Do I pass inspection, Your Majesty?" I ask playfully.

Tristan crosses the room in four strides, taking my hands in his. "You are…" He pauses, searching for words. "Magnificent."

Shannon discreetly slips from the room, leaving us in our private moment.

"The baby's been kicking all afternoon," I guide his hand to the side of my belly. "I think he knows we're going somewhere important."

"He?" Tristan raises an eyebrow. "Still convinced it's a boy?"

"Mother's intuition," I say with a confidence I don't entirely feel. We've chosen not to learn the sex, preferring to have one of life's few remaining surprises.

Tristan kneels before me, his hands framing my belly, lips pressing gently against the taut fabric.

"Boy or girl," he whispers, "you already have my heart."

My eyes sting with sudden tears. These moments—quiet, intimate, away from the cameras and the duties—are what make everything worthwhile. This is the Tristan only I get to see.

"We should go," I manage, blinking rapidly. "God forbid the queen makes the king late."

He rises, offering his arm. "Let them wait. The world revolves around you tonight."

◆━━━━━◆━━━━━◆

The grand ballroom of the National Museum glitters under chandeliers that have witnessed centuries of Haldonian history. Hundreds of candles cast a warm glow over tables adorned with white lilies and blue forget-me-nots—symbols of remembrance in our country. Every detail has been overseen personally by the gala committee, with Shannon acting as my proxy when my appointments wouldn't allow direct involvement.

As we enter, the orchestra transitions seamlessly into the royal anthem. Conversations pause, bodies turn, and heads bow in a synchronized display of respect that still makes my heart flutter nervously.

Parker, ever-present at Tristan's side, murmurs the evening's agenda into his ear as we move toward our designated table. I catch fragments—speeches, auction, ceremonial lighting—before my attention is diverted by a small group of children standing in formation near the stage.

"The choir," Shannon explains quietly from behind me. "Children who lost parents in the Crona War. They'll perform after dinner."

My grip on Tristan's arm tightens involuntarily, as I think about how it's going to affect us for years to come.

"You okay?" he asks, covering my hand with his.

I nod, focusing on maintaining my public smile. "Just wondering if these shoes were a mistake. My feet are already arguing with me."

He chuckles, but his eyes see through the deflection. "Two hours. Then we make our excuses."

"Three," I counter. "These children deserve our full attention."

The evening progresses with the precision of a well-rehearsed play. I sip water from crystal that matches everyone else's champagne flutes, accept condolences for my "sacrifice" of alcohol, and graciously receive countless hands on my belly as though it's become public property. Each touch, while well-intentioned, makes me increasingly grateful for Tristan's steady presence beside me.

During dinner, I notice him watching the children's choir with an intensity that suggests his mind is elsewhere. I've learned to recognize the look—part guilt, part responsibility—that overtakes him when confronted with the consequences of decisions made before his coronation but carried out under his early reign.

I place my hand on his knee beneath the table. "You're doing good work tonight," I whisper. "They know that."

His hand covers mine, squeezing gently. "I just hope it's enough."

When it's time for our address, we ascend the steps to the podium together. The teleprompter flickers to life, but Tristan sets aside the prepared remarks. I feel a momentary flash of panic—deviations from script make the communications team nervous—but trust him implicitly.

"Tonight," he begins, his voice carrying effortlessly across the hushed room, "we gather not merely as patrons or officials, but as a family united by loss and hope." His eyes scan the crowd, settling on the children. "To the Children of Heroes, I make this promise not as your king, but as someone who understands that no medal or monument can fill the void left by those you've lost."

A lump forms in my throat as he continues, speaking from experience and heart rather than political calculation.

When he finishes, I step forward, feeling the weight of all eyes upon me, upon us, upon the visible evidence of Haldonia's future growing beneath my heart.

"The foundation established tonight," I add, picking up where he left off, "will ensure that no child of a fallen service member will ever have to choose between opportunity and necessity. Education, healthcare, and housing assistance will be guaranteed." I rest my hand instinctively on my belly. "This is our covenant with you, from one generation to the next."

The applause is deafening, but it's the silent tears on young faces that tell me our words have found their mark.

Later, as the auction concludes and the final donations are tallied, I find myself seated at a table surrounded by children ranging from five to fifteen. My feet have indeed begun to protest the evening's demands, and I've discreetly slipped off my heels beneath the tablecloth.

"Is it a boy or a girl?" asks a small girl with solemn eyes and braids tied with blue ribbons.

"I don't know yet," I answer honestly. "What do you think it is?"

She considers this with surprising seriousness. "A boy. Kings need sons."

From across the table, an older boy shakes his head. "That's old-fashioned thinking, Elise. The queen could have a daughter who becomes the next ruler."

I smile at him, grateful for the progressive viewpoint. "That's absolutely right. Haldonia's constitution was amended before I married Tristan. Our child will be heir regardless of gender."

The conversation shifts to names, nursery colors, and whether the baby might have my eyes or Tristan's. These children, who have experienced loss beyond their years, still retain the capacity for wonder and curiosity that makes my heart ache with tenderness.

When Tristan finds me, he's accompanied by General Mercer, his father's most trusted military adviser and one of the few cabinet members retained after the coronation.

"Your Majesty," Mercer bows slightly. "You've captivated your subjects. The little ones haven't stopped talking about you."

"They're remarkable children," I reply, meaning it. "Resilient in ways I can barely comprehend."

As we exchange pleasantries, I notice Tristan's gaze continually drifting toward the exit. The subtle tension in his jaw tells me he's reaching his limit for public interaction tonight.

"I believe we should be going," I announce, allowing Tristan to help me to my feet. "The baby seems to think my ribs make an excellent punching bag tonight."

The general laughs, offering congratulations once more before Parker materializes to coordinate our departure.

The goodbyes take another thirty minutes—handshakes, promises to follow up, expressions of gratitude—before we finally make our way through the service entrance to where our vehicle waits.

The night air feels glorious after hours in the crowded ballroom. I inhale deeply, savoring the cool September breeze as Parker opens the door to the Range Rover.

"Successful evening," I comment as Tristan slides in beside me.

He loosens his collar, exhaling slowly. "The foundation exceeded its funding goal. Parker says the initial social media response is overwhelmingly positive."

"And you connected with them," I add, taking his hand. "The children, I mean. They saw you, not just the crown."

His thumb traces circles on my palm, a gentle, absent gesture that speaks of comfort and familiarity. "You were the star tonight. 'The queen's maternal glow' will dominate tomorrow's headlines."

"God, I hope not," I groan, settling back against the leather seat as our driver navigates through the museum's service exit. "I'd rather they focus on the record donation amounts."

The route back to the palace is familiar—first the cultural district, through the diplomatic quarter, past Parliament Square before entering the palace grounds through the eastern gate. But tonight, as we approach the central boulevard, I notice Parker shift in the front passenger seat, his posture suddenly alert.

"Sir," our driver's voice carries an edge I've rarely heard. "There's unusual activity ahead."

Through the tinted windows, I can make out a gathering crowd near the square. Banners and signs wave in the darkness, illuminated sporadically by streetlights and the harsh glow of smartphone screens.

"Protesters," Parker confirms, already on his phone. "Security wasn't expecting this tonight. They're mobilizing units from the palace now."

"What are they protesting?" I ask, leaning forward to better see.

Tristan's hand on my arm pulls me gently back. "The war," he says quietly. They're still angry that we fought back. The people out here want nothing more than peace."

My stomach clenches with understanding. The Children of Heroes gala, while well-intentioned, would be seen by some as glorifying a conflict many believed unnecessary. The timing suddenly seems tone-deaf, despite the months of planning.

"We should go around," Parker instructs the driver. "Take Parliament Road to—"

His words cut off as our vehicle slows dramatically. Through the front windshield, I can see that the road ahead has been blocked by a makeshift barricade—trash bins, bikes, and what looks like construction materials dragged from a nearby site.

"Backing up," our driver announces calmly, but as the Range Rover begins to reverse, the rear view shows more protesters moving in behind us.

"They're boxing us in," Parker says, his voice professionally even despite the implication. He's back on his phone, urgency evident in his clipped sentences.

Beside me, Tristan has gone completely still. His hand, still holding mine, has turned ice cold.

"It's okay," I tell him, though my heart hammers against my ribs. "Security will be here any minute."

But Tristan doesn't seem to hear me. His eyes have taken on a vacant quality that sends a chill down my spine. I've seen this look only once before, when fireworks at the National Day celebration triggered something in him that took hours to subside.

"Tristan," I say more firmly, squeezing his hand. "Look at me."

The crowd is closing in now, faces pressed against the windows, signs thumping against metal and glass. Our vehicle's bulletproof design suddenly seems both reassuring and claustrophobic.

"Ambush," Tristan whispers, so softly I almost miss it. His breathing has become shallow, rapid. "Just like Northpoint. They waited until the convoy was surrounded."

My blood runs cold. Northpoint—the worst massacre of the Northern Conflict, where Tristan's unit lost seventeen men in a single afternoon. He rarely speaks of it, but I know from his nightmares that the memories remain vivid.

"Tristan, we're in the capital," I say, keeping my voice steady despite the fear building in my chest. "This is a protest, not combat. Look at me, please."

His eyes lock onto mine, but I'm not sure he's seeing me. His free hand has moved instinctively to where a sidearm would be if he were in combat gear rather than formal dress.

The baby chooses this moment to deliver a particularly strong kick, making me gasp involuntarily. The sound seems to penetrate whatever fog has enveloped Tristan. His focus sharpens, concern replacing the distant terror in his eyes.

"Lia," he says, my nickname a lifeline pulling him back. "Are you hurt?"

"We're fine," I assure him, deliberately placing his hand on my belly where our child continues its gymnastic routine. "We're both fine. Just scared."

The contact seems to ground him. I watch as awareness returns fully, his military training reasserting itself as he assesses our situation with renewed clarity.

"Parker," he calls to the front seat. "Status?"

"Palace security is two minutes out," Parker reports. "Metropolitan police are establishing a perimeter. The protesters appear to be unarmed, just agitated."

Through the window, I can make out their chants now. Not threats against us personally, but anger about the war, demands for accountability, calls for reparations to the northern provinces.

Tristan's arm wraps around my shoulders, drawing me against him in a protective gesture that feels more instinctive than calculated.

"I'm sorry," he murmurs against my hair. "I was…somewhere else for a moment."

"I know," I whisper back. "But you came back to me. You always do."

The distant wail of sirens grows louder, and the crowd's enthusiasm noticeably dampens. Within minutes, uniformed officers create a pathway through the protesters, and our vehicle begins moving slowly toward the palace.

As we pass through the dissipating crowd, I catch glimpses of their faces—angry, yes, but also wounded, grieving, seeking acknowledgment of losses that no gala or foundation can truly address. These are Tristan's subjects too, their pain as valid as the children we just honored.

"We need to listen to them," I say quietly.

Tristan nods, his composure fully restored though his arm remains firmly around me. "Yes," he agrees. "Not tonight, but soon. They deserve that much."

By the time we reach the palace gates, my feet have swollen painfully in my discarded shoes, and exhaustion weighs on me like a physical burden. But as we're escorted through private corridors to our chambers, I find myself reflecting on the contrast of the evening—the glittering ballroom versus the raw emotion of the streets.

This is the complexity of loving a king, of being a queen. The beautiful and the terrible exist side by side, the formal duties and the human costs, the public expectation and the private struggles.

In our bedroom, as Shannon helps me out of my gown and Tristan confers with security about tomorrow's response, I catch his eye across the room. Despite everything—the flashback, the protesters, the weight of responsibilities that never lightens—he smiles at me with such tenderness that my breath catches.

Later, as we lie together in the darkness, his hand resting protectively over our child, I realize that this is what makes our love story real. Not the fairy tale trappings or royal titles, but the way we anchor each other through storms, the way we recognize each other's fractures and hold them gently.

"Do you ever wish for a simpler life?" I ask into the quiet.

His lips brush my forehead, and I feel him smile against my skin. "Never," he answers without hesitation. "Not if it meant a life without you."

And despite the fears that linger, despite knowing that tomorrow will bring new challenges and complications, I believe him completely.

CHAPTER 24
TRISTAN

The light is fading by the time we make it back to our quarters. My body aches from tension, muscles still rigid from the crowd we faced earlier. Even after all these months as king, I'm still not used to the protesters, the press of bodies, the unpredictable movements and shouts. Today was particularly intense. The weight of the day hangs heavy on my shoulders as I push open the door, immediately loosening my tie.

Lia follows me in, her face etched with concern she's been trying to hide since we left the square. She's changed quickly out of her formal attire, wearing just a simple tank top and those soft cotton pants that make her look impossibly young.

"Kate called," I say, discarding my jacket and draping it over the back of a chair. "Got my schedule sorted for an early departure on Friday."

Lia's expression brightens slightly. "The beach house?" There's hope in her voice, and I nod, watching her eyes light up.

"Leaving at eleven." I reach for her, needing to touch her, to ground myself in her presence. My hands settle at her waist, and I draw her close, breathing in the scent of her hair as she tucks herself against me.

"Good. We need it." She presses her face into my chest, and I feel her body relax against mine.

"You okay?" I ask, running my hands up and down her back.

She pulls back, looking up at me with disbelief. "Shouldn't I be asking you that? That crowd today was..." She shakes her head, unable to find the right words.

"Just doing my job," I say, aiming for lightness but probably missing by a mile.

She studies my face intently. "You look exhausted, Tris."

I try to smile, but I can feel it falter. No point in lying to her. She reads me too well. "It takes a lot out of me. More than I like to admit."

She takes my hand and leads me to the couch, tugging me down beside her. We sit in silence for a moment, her fingers intertwined with mine.

"I was scared for you today," she admits finally. "When that man broke through the barricade and security tackled him. You didn't even flinch."

I shrug, aiming for nonchalance but probably missing by a mile. "Years of practice."

She shifts to face me fully, tucking one leg beneath her. "How do you do that? Stay so calm in the chaos." Her voice drops lower. "Since the war...since your PTSD...I've seen how crowds affect you. But today, you never even showed a sign of having a complete breakdown."

The question makes me pause. Lia has seen me at my worst, has talked me through the nightmares, has held me when the memories become too much. But today was different—a public challenge in front of hundreds of angry citizens, cameras capturing every reaction.

I reach into my pocket and pull out the small brass object I carried through the protest. "This helps," I say, placing my grandfather's compass in her palm.

She examines it carefully, running her thumb over the worn surface. "Your grandfather's compass? I've seen you holding it before, but I didn't know..."

"He gave it to me before my first deployment." I watch as she opens it, the needle swinging gently before settling. "Said no matter how lost I felt, this would help me find my way home."

"It's beautiful," she murmurs.

"When things get bad, when I feel myself starting to spiral, I hold on to it." I close my hand over hers, feeling the compass between our palms. "I focus on the weight of it, the texture. I remind myself where I am, who I am now."

She looks up at me, her eyes shining with unshed tears. "Does it work?"

"Most of the time." I take the compass back, closing it with a soft click. "But I love having you more."

She cups my face in her hands, her touch so gentle it almost undoes me. "I wish I could take it all away. The pain, the memories."

I turn my head to press a kiss to her palm. "I don't. They're part of me, part of what made me the man I am now. I wouldn't change that."

Lia leans forward, resting her forehead against mine. "I love you," she whispers. "Every broken piece, every scar, every triumph. All of you."

"Even when I wake you at ungodly hours because of nightmares?"

Her smile is soft, intimate. "Especially then. Because that's when you let me see you—really see you."

I kiss her then, slow and deep, trying to pour into it everything I can't find words for. My gratitude, my devotion, my endless wonder that she chose me.

We stay like that, trading kisses and quiet confessions, until exhaustion begins to claim us both. The day has been long, and we still have the rest of the week to get through before our escape to the beach house.

"Bed?" I suggest, and she nods, stifling a yawn.

Our nighttime routine is comfortable, familiar. We move around each other in the bathroom, brushing teeth, washing faces. Lia braids her hair while I change into sleep pants. There's something profoundly intimate about these mundane moments that still catches me off guard —the easy domesticity of it all.

When we finally slide between the sheets, Lia immediately curls into my side, her head on my chest, her arm draped across my waist. I wrap my arms around her, holding her close.

"Think you'll sleep tonight?" she murmurs, already drifting.

"With you here? Always better odds." I press a kiss to her forehead.

She makes a soft sound of contentment, and within minutes, her breathing evens out. I lie awake a little longer, listening to the rhythm of her breaths, feeling the warmth of her body against mine. In these quiet moments, the weight I carry as king seems to lift, if only temporarily. Here, I am simply a man holding the woman he loves.

I must drift off eventually because the next thing I know, I'm jerking awake, heart pounding. Not a nightmare this time, but a dream so vivid it leaves me disoriented. Lia. It was about Lia, about losing her, about reaching for her across an impossible distance.

I turn my head to find her still sleeping beside me, her face peaceful in the moonlight filtering through the curtains. The relief is immediate and overwhelming. She's here. She's safe. She's mine.

The need to touch her, to feel her alive and warm against me, is suddenly urgent. I roll onto my side, running my hand lightly over the curve of her hip. She stirs but doesn't wake, and I lean in to press my lips to the sensitive spot just below her ear.

"Lia," I whisper, my voice rough with sleep and need. "Lia, wake up."

She makes a soft sound of protest, eyes still closed. "Hmm?"

I trail kisses down her neck, my hand slipping beneath her sleep shirt to find the warm skin beneath. "Need you," I murmur against her skin.

She turns toward me then, eyes blinking open, confused but not alarmed. "Tris? What time is it?"

"Don't know. Don't care." I capture her mouth with mine, pouring all my desperation, all my love into the kiss. When I pull back, her eyes are fully open now, alert and darkening with desire. "I just need to feel close to you. Need to know you're real."

Understanding softens her features. She reaches up to touch my face, her fingers tracing the line of my jaw. "I'm here," she says simply. "I'm right here."

Her hands slide into my hair, drawing me down for another kiss, this one deeper, hungrier. My body responds instantly, every nerve ending alive with want. I move over her, my weight supported on my forearms, and she parts her legs to cradle me between them.

"Love you," I breathe against her lips. "Love you so much it terrifies me sometimes."

She answers not with words but with her body, arching up against me, her hands pulling me closer. There's an urgency between us now, a desperate need to connect, to reaffirm what we have.

We move together in the darkness, clothing discarded, hands mapping familiar territory as if discovering it anew. Every touch, every kiss is both a question and an answer. Are you with me? I am here. Do you feel this? With every fiber of my being.

When we finally join, the sense of completeness is overwhelming. I pause, forehead pressed to hers, just breathing her in. Her hands clutch at my shoulders, her eyes locked with mine, and in that moment, everything else falls away. There is no kingdom, no crown, no past trauma or future uncertainty. There is only this—only us.

"You are my home," I tell her as we begin to move together. "My true north."

Her answer is my name on her lips, a prayer and a promise all at once.

Later, as we lie tangled together, her head on my chest and my arms wrapped securely around her, I feel the lingering tension finally release its hold. The compass rests on the nightstand beside us, but I find I don't need it now. Not when I'm holding my heart in my arms.

"Better?" Lia asks softly, pressing a kiss to my chest, right over my heart.

I tighten my arms around her. "Perfect," I reply, and for this moment at least, it's nothing but the truth.

CHAPTER 25
AMELIA

I stand in the doorway of what was once a spare bedroom, marveling at the transformation. Soft yellow walls, a white crib with delicate linens, a rocking chair by the window overlooking the palace gardens —it's perfect. Well, almost perfect.

"What do you think about moving the bookshelf closer to the rocking chair?" I ask, rubbing my swollen belly as I feel a tiny foot or elbow push against my palm.

Tristan looks up from where he's arranging stuffed animals in the crib—a task I find endlessly endearing. The King of Haldonia, meticulously positioning a plush elephant next to a giraffe, his brow furrowed in concentration.

"That makes sense," he says, straightening. "That way you can reach for a book while you're nursing."

My heart swells at his thoughtfulness. Eight months pregnant, and I still can't believe this is my life sometimes. Queen of Haldonia, married to a man who looks at me like I hung the moon and about to become a mother.

"Do you think we're ready?" I ask, the question slipping out before I can stop it.

Tristan crosses the room and wraps his arms around me from behind, his hands joining mine on my belly. "Absolutely not," he murmurs against my ear, his voice warm with humor. "But I don't think anyone ever is."

I lean back against his chest, soaking in his strength. "At least we have the nursery ready."

"Almost ready," he corrects. "I still need to add the security features Parker insists on."

I roll my eyes. "Our baby doesn't need panic buttons before they're even born."

"Parker disagrees. And you know how he gets when we argue with him about security."

I do know. Our head of security is fiercely protective, especially now that there's a royal baby on the way. Sometimes I find it stifling, but mostly I'm grateful. The world we live in comes with risks, and Parker helps us navigate them.

"We should finish up," I say reluctantly. "The guests will be arriving soon."

Tristan groans dramatically. "Do we have to? Can't we just tell everyone the shower is canceled and spend the day in here instead?"

I turn in his arms, looking up at him. "Nice try. My mother has been planning this for weeks. She'll hunt us down if we try to skip out."

"Your mother is terrifying," he says with a smile that tells me he adores her.

"She is," I agree. "Now help me move this bookshelf, Your Majesty, before I'm too tired to enjoy our own baby shower."

The grand salon has been transformed with tasteful decorations in soft greens and yellows. No gendered colors since we've decided to wait until birth to learn whether we're having a son or daughter. Elegant flower arrangements, delicate refreshments, and a table piled with wrapped gifts dominate the space.

"Amelia, darling!" My mother glides toward me, elegant as always in a pale blue dress that complements her silver hair. "You look radiant."

"I feel enormous," I confess as she embraces me.

"Nonsense. You're carrying the future of Haldonia. There's nothing more beautiful." She steps back, surveying me with the critical eye that used to make me squirm as a teenager. Now I find it comforting. "Although you might want to sit down. Your ankles are starting to swell."

Some things never change.

"Mom, please try to remember I'm a grown woman. And a queen."

"And still my daughter." She pats my cheek affectionately before turning to greet Shannon, who approaches with a glass of sparkling water for me.

"Your Majesty," Shannon says with a wink. My personal assistant and friend, she's one of the few people who helps me feel normal in this extraordinary life.

"Don't you start," I warn, accepting the drink gratefully.

"Rough morning?" she asks, her voice lowered so only I can hear.

"Just the usual. Backache, swollen feet, and a husband who hovers like I might break if he looks away for too long."

Shannon laughs. "He's adorable when he's worried about you."

"Don't encourage him." But I can't help smiling as I spot Tristan across the room, deep in conversation with Kate, his assistant. Even from here, I can see he's gesturing toward me, probably giving her instructions about clearing his schedule further as my due date approaches.

More guests arrive—palace staff who have become like family, a few trusted friends from before my royal life, some dignitaries who couldn't be excluded without causing diplomatic incidents. The room fills with conversation and laughter.

I settle into a comfortable chair that someone (undoubtedly Tristan) has positioned perfectly for me to see everything without being over-whelmed by well-wishers. As if summoned by my thoughts, he appears beside me, perching on the arm of my chair.

"Are you comfortable? Do you need anything?" he asks, his voice low.

"I'm fine," I assure him, squeezing his hand. "Go mingle. Be kingly."

He snorts. "I'd rather be husbandly."

"Later," I promise with a meaningful look that makes his eyes darken. Even with my enormous belly between us, the chemistry hasn't faded.

The shower proceeds with games (tasteful ones, thankfully—my mother knows I'd never forgive her for anything involving melted chocolate in diapers), gift opening, and food. Through it all, Tristan never strays far from my side, and I catch myself watching him more than once.

He's changed since we met. Still the same strong, sometimes stubborn man, but softer around the edges now. More willing to laugh, to show vulnerability. I'd like to think I've had something to do with that transformation, just as he's helped me grow more confident in my role as queen.

"Earth to Amelia," Shannon says, waving a hand in front of my face. "Lost in thought?"

"Just thinking about how much has changed," I admit. "Back when all this first started, I had no idea what was waiting for me. I was nervous as hell to meet Tristan, and thought he'd be so cold. I had an allowance, and I was supposed to myself pure for my new role."

"Now you're opening gifts worth more than my annual salary?" She gestures to the antique silver rattle I've just unwrapped from the Ambassador of France.

"Now I'm preparing to raise a child in a castle," I correct her. "It's surreal."

"You're going to be an amazing mother," Shannon says with such conviction that I blink back sudden tears.

"Sorry," I say, dabbing at my eyes. "Hormones."

"Blame everything on hormones while you can," she advises. "It's the one perk of pregnancy everyone can agree on."

The afternoon wears on, and I find myself genuinely enjoying the celebration despite my earlier reluctance. Watching Tristan's face as we open each gift—his confusion over some of the more obscure baby items, his genuine delight at the handmade blanket from Kate, his touched expression when my mother presents us with my own preserved baby booties—fills me with a happiness so intense it's almost painful.

As the event winds down, I find myself seated between my mother and Tristan, watching the remaining guests chat in small groups.

"I never thought I'd see this day," my mother says softly, her hand covering mine.

"Me becoming a mother?" I ask.

"You being so completely happy," she corrects me. "I always knew you'd be a wonderful mother when the time came. But this"—she gestures around the room, at the life I've built— "this exceeds even my highest hopes for you."

I lean my head against her shoulder, feeling for a moment like a little girl again. "Thank you for being here for all of it."

"I wouldn't be anywhere else." She kisses the top of my head, then stands. "Now, I think you need to rest before you fall asleep right here. Tristan, take my daughter to bed."

"Mom!" I protest, feeling my cheeks heat.

"To sleep," she clarifies with a knowing smile that makes me blush deeper. "Though what you do before sleeping is none of my business."

Tristan, to his credit, manages to keep a straight face as he helps me to my feet. "Yes, ma'am."

As we make our way out of the salon, I lean against him, suddenly exhausted but content. Our baby is loved, not just by us but by an entire community of people who will help us raise them. A village, royal style.

"Did you have a good time?" Tristan asks as we walk slowly toward our private wing.

"Better than I expected," I admit. "Though I'm ready to be alone with you now."

He tightens his arm around my waist. "Just wait until you see what I've done with the nursery while you were distracted."

"What do you mean?" I ask, curious despite my fatigue.

"I may have added one more thing while you were busy with your mother before the shower."

When we reach the nursery, he guides me inside and flips a switch I hadn't noticed before. The ceiling transforms into a night sky, stars twinkling softly overhead.

"Oh, Tristan," I breathe, tilting my head back to take in the constellations. "It's beautiful."

"I thought we could teach our little one about the stars," he says, watching my face anxiously. "Do you like it?"

In answer, I pull him down for a kiss, pouring all my love and gratitude into it. When we part, both a little breathless, I whisper, "It's perfect. Everything is perfect."

And in this moment, despite the aches and uncertainties, despite the pressures of royal life and the challenges of impending parenthood, I mean it. Everything is perfect.

CHAPTER 26
TRISTAN

"Are you sure about this?" I ask Amelia for the third time as Parker pulls the car to a stop in front of an unremarkable community center. "We could have arranged for private lessons."

Lia rolls her eyes at me, a gesture I've come to both love and dread. "We've been over this. I want our baby to have as normal a life as possible. That starts with us taking a regular Lamaze class like regular parents."

"We're not regular parents," I point out, though I know it's a losing battle. "I'm the King of Haldonia, and you're—"

"Currently very pregnant and not interested in arguing," she cuts me off with a sweet smile that doesn't fool me for a second. "Come on, we're going to be late."

Parker catches my eye in the rearview mirror, his expression carefully neutral but with a hint of amusement he can't quite hide. "I've checked the building, sir. The instructor has been vetted, and there are two agents already inside posing as another expectant couple."

"See?" Amelia says triumphantly. "Parker has it all under control. Now help me out of this car before I have to roll myself out."

I exit and circle around to her side, offering my hand as she leverages her eight-month pregnant body from the vehicle. Even with her belly leading the way and her ankles slightly swollen, she's the most beautiful woman I've ever seen. My queen in every sense of the word.

"You know the security protocol," Parker reminds us as we head toward the entrance. "If I say the word 'fireplace,' we leave immediately. No questions, no goodbyes."

"Yes, Parker," we say in unison, the routine familiar after years of his protection.

The community center smells like floor cleaner and coffee. A hand-lettered sign directs us to "Lamaze with Linda—Room 3," and we follow the arrow down a hallway lined with community announcements and children's artwork.

"This is nice," Amelia says, her hand firmly in mine. "Reminds me of where I used to volunteer before we met."

I make a noncommittal sound, taking everything in with the heightened awareness I've developed since becoming king. Old habits from my military days resurface whenever I'm in an unfamiliar environment. Exits, potential threats, line of sight to Parker who trails a few steps behind us—I catalog it all automatically.

Room 3 is a large, airy space with yoga mats and pillows arranged in a circle. Five other couples are already there, chatting among themselves. When we enter, the conversation stops abruptly, followed by the widened eyes and sharp intakes of breath I've come to expect.

"Your Majesties." A woman in her fifties with gray-streaked hair pulled into a bun approaches us, her composure admirable. "I'm Linda. Welcome to my class. I'm honored to have you join us."

"Thank you for having us," Amelia says warmly. "Please, I'm just Amelia here, and this is Tristan. We're here to learn, just like everyone else."

Linda's smile grows more genuine. "Of course. Why don't you find a spot and get comfortable? We'll be starting in a few minutes once everyone arrives."

We settle onto a mat near the edge of the circle, giving Parker a clear view of the door. I help Amelia arrange pillows behind her back, acutely aware of the stares and whispers from the other couples.

"They'll get over it," she murmurs to me, reading my discomfort as easily as she always does.

"It's not too late to leave," I offer half-heartedly.

She pats my knee. "Nice try. Now smile and look approachable."

I make an effort to relax my face, which Amelia tells me can look intimidating when I'm thinking too hard. The couple nearest to us—a young man with a sleeve of tattoos and a woman with vibrant blue hair—exchange glances before the woman takes a deep breath and turns toward us.

"I just want to say, Your Majesty—I mean, Amelia—that your education initiative has made a huge difference at the school where I teach. Because of the funding, we now have a proper music program."

Amelia's face lights up. "That's wonderful to hear. Music education was one of my passions before..." She gestures around us, encompassing the life change that brought her to the throne.

"I know," the woman says with a shy smile. "I read your dissertation on the impact of arts education on academic achievement."

"You did?" Amelia looks genuinely surprised and delighted.

"I cited it in my master's thesis," the woman admits. "I never thought I'd get to thank you in person."

I watch as my wife engages in animated conversation about educational theory, the initial awkwardness melting away. This is what makes her such an extraordinary queen—her genuine interest in people and causes, her ability to connect on a human level despite the crown she wears.

By the time Linda calls the class to order, the atmosphere has shifted. We're still the royal couple, but we're also just Tristan and Amelia, nervous first-time parents like everyone else in the room.

"All right, everyone," Linda begins, "today we're focusing on breathing techniques and positions that can help during labor. Partners, your job is incredibly important. You're the anchor, the support, the coach who helps keep mom focused when things get intense."

I straighten, taking the responsibility as seriously as I take running a country. Amelia catches my expression and suppresses a smile.

"First, let's have the moms get comfortable in a supported sitting position," Linda instructs. "Partners, you'll sit behind them, providing back support."

I position myself behind Amelia, my legs on either side of her, her back against my chest. The position feels oddly vulnerable here in this public space, but also right. This is where I belong—supporting her, being her strength when she needs it.

"Now, let's practice some deep breathing," Linda continues. "In through the nose for four counts, out through the mouth for six."

We breathe together, my chest rising and falling in sync with Amelia's. The rhythm is calming, meditative, and I find myself relaxing into the experience despite my initial reservations.

The class progresses through various positions and techniques. When Linda demonstrates how to apply counter-pressure during contractions, I listen with intense concentration, determined to get it exactly right. Amelia winces when I press too hard on her lower back.

"Sorry," I whisper, immediately easing off.

"It's okay," she assures me. "Just maybe don't approach my spine like you're defending the realm from invasion."

The tattooed man next to us chuckles. "First time I tried that on Zoey, she nearly took my head off."

"Men," Zoey says with an affectionate eye roll that reminds me of Amelia. "They either go way too gentle or act like they're kneading bread dough."

"Exactly!" Amelia agrees, and suddenly we're part of a universal conversation about the challenges of pregnancy and partnership that transcends our royal status.

By the time we move on to massage techniques, I've forgotten to be self-conscious. When Linda suggests the fathers try massaging their partners' shoulders, I focus entirely on Amelia, working my thumbs into the knots I know she carries from hours of reading briefing documents.

She sighs appreciatively, leaning into my touch. "You should add 'royal masseur' to your list of titles," she murmurs.

"Only for you," I reply, dropping a kiss on the top of her head.

The rest of the class flies by in a blur of information, practice, and surprisingly genuine connection with the other couples. When Linda concludes the session, I'm almost disappointed it's over.

"Next week, we'll go over more advanced techniques and start discussing birth plans," Linda announces. "Great work today, everyone."

As we gather our things, several couples approach us, the initial awe replaced by the camaraderie of shared experience.

"Do you know if you're having a boy or girl?" one woman asks Amelia.

"We're waiting to find out," she replies, her hand finding mine. "Tristan thinks it's a girl, but I'm not convinced."

"Mother's intuition says boy?" another father-to-be asks me.

"She thinks it's a boy, and she'll tell anyone who asks," I grin.

"I do not!" Amelia protests, then pauses. "Do I?"

"Constantly," I confirm, enjoying her surprise.

We say our goodbyes with promises to return next week, and I'm surprised to find I'm looking forward to it. As we walk back to the car where Parker waits, Amelia bumps her shoulder against my arm.

"Admit it," she says smugly. "You had fun."

"It was educational," I concede, trying to maintain some dignity.

"You exchanged phone numbers with Tattoo Guy."

"Miguel," I correct her. "And it's good to have connections outside the palace."

She laughs, the sound bright in the evening air. "I knew you'd like it if you gave it a chance."

As Parker opens the car door for us, Amelia suddenly stops. "Wait," she says, her eyes widening with sudden longing. "Ice cream."

"Ice cream?" I repeat, glancing at my watch. It's nearly nine, and most shops will be closed.

"I need chocolate ice cream," she says with the seriousness of a state declaration. "With caramel sauce. And maybe pecans."

I look at Parker, who's already on his phone. After a brief conversation, he turns to us. "There's a shop three blocks from here. The owner is willing to reopen for Your Majesties."

"You're a miracle worker, Parker," Amelia tells him with sincere gratitude.

"Just doing my job, ma'am."

Twenty minutes later, we're seated in an empty ice cream parlor, the owner hovering nervously as Amelia devours a massive sundae with evident bliss. I pick at my own much smaller vanilla cone, more entertained by her enjoyment than interested in the dessert.

"This," she announces between bites, "is exactly what I needed after all that breathing and stretching."

"The royal heir demands ice cream?" I tease.

"The royal heir's mother demands ice cream," she corrects me. "The baby just benefits from my happiness."

I reach across the table to wipe a spot of chocolate from the corner of her mouth. "Your happiness is my primary concern, you know."

Her expression softens. "I know. That's why I love you." She glances around the small shop, at Parker standing discreetly by the door, at the owner pretending not to stare from behind the counter. "And this—normal moments stolen in the midst of our very abnormal life—this is what makes me happy."

"Then we'll have more of them," I promise. "Ice cream runs, Lamaze classes, whatever you want."

"Whatever I want?" She raises an eyebrow, a mischievous gleam in her eye. "That's a dangerous offer to make to a hormonal woman with royal authority."

I lean forward, dropping my voice so only she can hear. "I'm not afraid of you."

"You should be," she whispers back, but her smile tells me everything I need to know.

In this moment, king and queen are secondary titles. We're just Tristan and Amelia, sharing ice cream on a weeknight, preparing for our baby, stealing normal in the midst of extraordinary. And I wouldn't have it any other way.

CHAPTER 27
AMELIA

Something isn't right.

I've been feeling off for the past couple of days—more tired than usual, a persistent backache that won't ease no matter how I sit, occasional twinges that I've been dismissing as Braxton Hicks contractions. But this morning, the discomfort has taken on a different quality.

"Your Majesty?" The Minister of Education pauses in the middle of her presentation, looking at me with concern. "Are you all right?"

I realize I've been rubbing my lower back and grimacing. "I'm fine," I assure her, straightening in my chair. "Please continue."

She returns to her discussion of rural school funding, but I find it increasingly difficult to focus. My back is really hurting now, a deep, rhythmic ache that seems to wrap around to my abdomen every fifteen minutes or so.

I glance at my watch. Tristan is in the northern province today, touring flood damage and meeting with local officials. He's not due back until evening. I should call him, I think, then immediately dismiss the idea. This is probably nothing. No need to pull him away from important work just because I'm uncomfortable.

Shannon catches my eye from her position near the door, her brow furrowed in question. I give her a small smile that I hope is reassuring, though judging by her expression, I'm not convincing anyone.

Another pain grips me, stronger this time, making me inhale sharply. The minister stops again, and even the most oblivious of my advisers are now watching me with concern.

"Perhaps we should continue this meeting another time," Shannon suggests smoothly, already moving to my side.

"No, I—" I begin to protest, then feel a distinct pop and a rush of warm fluid between my legs. Oh. Oh no.

The room falls silent as everyone realizes what's happening. I look down at the puddle forming beneath my chair, momentarily frozen in disbelief. I'm only thirty-eight weeks along. This wasn't supposed to happen for another two weeks, when Tristan would be firmly by my side.

"Call the hospital," Shannon commands, her voice cutting through my shock. "And get Parker. The queen is in labor."

The next few minutes are a blur of activity. Someone helps me to my feet. Shannon disappears briefly, returning with a change of clothes. Parker materializes, his usual stoic expression replaced by alert efficiency. Typically he would be with Tristan, but because I'm so close to my due date, Parker has been assigned to me.

"We need to get you to the hospital, Your Majesty," he says, already guiding me toward the door. "The car is waiting."

"Tristan," I manage to say as another contraction builds. "Call Tristan."

"Already done," Shannon assures me, supporting me on my other side. "He's on his way back. The helicopter was already standing by."

The knowledge that he's coming should reassure me, but suddenly the reality of what's happening crashes down. I'm having a baby. Today. Now. And Tristan is hours away.

"I can't do this without him," I whisper to Shannon as we make our way slowly down the corridor.

"You won't have to," she promises. "He'll be there."

But we both know labor can progress quickly. The rush of fear makes my knees weak.

Parker and Shannon help me into the waiting car, and we're

speeding toward the hospital with a police escort before I fully process what's happening. The contractions are coming faster now, about ten minutes apart, each one stealing my breath.

"Try to breathe through them," Shannon coaches, demonstrating the techniques we learned in Lamaze class. "In through your nose, out through your mouth."

I try to follow her example, but panic is making it difficult. "It's too early," I say between contractions. "The nursery isn't completely ready. Tristan's speech for the announcement isn't finalized. I haven't packed a hospital bag."

"Everything is taken care of," she assures me, her calm voice anchoring me. "Kate had your bag prepared weeks ago, and the hospital has been on standby since your thirty-sixth week. The royal suite is ready."

Of course it is. In my rational mind, I know the palace operates with military precision. But right now, I don't feel like a queen with an army of staff ensuring everything runs smoothly. I feel like a scared first-time mother whose husband isn't here.

"Shannon." I grab her hand as another contraction builds, this one strong enough to make me gasp. "I'm scared."

She squeezes my fingers, her expression softening. "I know. But you're the strongest person I know, Amelia. You've handled ambassadors, state dinners, and Tristan at his worst. You can absolutely handle this."

Her mention of Tristan makes tears spring to my eyes. "What if he doesn't make it in time?"

"He will," she says with such conviction that I almost believe her. "But even if he's cutting it close, I'll be with you every step of the way. I promise."

The car pulls up to the private entrance of the hospital, where a medical team is already waiting. Everything happens with practiced efficiency—I'm whisked into a wheelchair, brought through corridors cleared of other patients, and settled into a spacious suite that looks more like a luxury hotel room than a hospital.

A doctor examines me while nurses hook up monitors that track the baby's heartbeat and my contractions. The steady thrum of our child's heart fills the room, momentarily distracting me from my fear.

"You're at four centimeters, Your Majesty," the doctor informs me. "Making good progress, but we still have some time. The baby's heart rate is excellent, and everything looks normal despite being a bit early."

"How much time?" I ask, thinking only of Tristan.

"First labors typically last twelve to twenty-four hours," she says gently. "Though every woman is different. I wouldn't expect this baby before late tonight at the earliest."

Relief washes over me. Surely Tristan will be here by then. Shannon's phone buzzes, and she steps away to answer it, returning moments later with a smile.

"That was Parker. Tristan's helicopter just landed at the palace. He'll be here within twenty minutes."

Twenty minutes. I can handle anything for twenty minutes. As if to challenge this resolve, another contraction seizes me, stronger than any before. I grip the bedrails, trying to remember my breathing, but a moan escapes me anyway.

Shannon takes my hand, letting me squeeze as the pain peaks, then gradually subsides. "You're doing great," she encourages.

"This hurts more than I expected," I admit once I can speak again.

"Do you want to discuss pain management options?" the doctor asks. "We have everything available, from an epidural to—"

"Not yet," I interrupt. "I want to wait for Tristan."

She nods understandingly. "Of course. I'll check back in an hour unless you need me sooner."

As the medical team steps out, leaving just Shannon and me with a nurse monitoring the machines, I feel another wave of vulnerability wash over me.

"What if I'm terrible at this?" I ask Shannon, voicing the fear that's been lingering beneath the surface for months. "At being a mother, I mean."

She sits on the edge of my bed, her expression serious. "Do you remember last year when that five-year-old girl presented you with flowers at the children's hospital? She was so nervous she dropped them, and you got down on your knees in that ridiculously expensive gown to help her pick them up."

I nod, remembering the child's trembling lip and my instinctive desire to comfort her.

"Or the time you stayed up all night with the ambassador's teenage daughter when she was having a crisis about her future? Or how you personally revamped the entire royal education initiative because you didn't think it was serving children properly?"

"That's different," I protest. "That's just being decent."

"That's being a natural nurturer," Shannon corrects me. "You care, Amelia. Deeply and genuinely. That's the most important quality in a parent."

Before I can respond, the door bursts open, and Tristan rushes in, still wearing his coat, his hair disheveled as if he's been running his hands through it.

"Lia!" he exclaims, immediately coming to my side and taking my hand. "Are you all right? Is the baby okay?"

The sight of him—worried, slightly rumpled, completely focused on me—releases something tight in my chest. "We're both fine," I assure him. "You made it."

"Of course I made it," he says, pressing his lips to my forehead. "I told the pilot I'd take over if he didn't get me here in time."

The mental image of Tristan attempting to fly a helicopter makes me laugh despite everything. "I'm sure that went over well."

"He seemed to take the threat seriously," Tristan says with a small smile, his thumb stroking the back of my hand.

Shannon rises from her spot on the bed. "I'll give you two some privacy. I'll be right outside if you need anything."

"Shannon," I call as she reaches the door. She turns back, and I try to convey everything I'm feeling with my eyes. "Thank you."

She nods, understanding all I'm not saying, and slips out.

Tristan takes her place on the edge of the bed, his eyes scanning my face. "How are you really doing?"

"Scared," I admit, knowing I don't need to pretend with him. "Excited. In pain. All of the above."

"I'm sorry I wasn't there when it started," he says, guilt clouding his features.

"You're here now," I tell him, squeezing his hand. "That's what matters."

Another contraction begins to build, and I tense, gripping his hand tighter. "Talk to me," I manage to say between clenched teeth. "Distract me."

He launches into a story about his helicopter ride, how he practically ordered the pilot to break speed records, how Parker kept trying to remind him of security protocols while Tristan was focused solely on getting to me. His voice anchors me as the pain crests and recedes.

"Better?" he asks as I relax back against the pillows.

"For now," I say, catching my breath. "They're getting stronger."

He brushes a strand of hair from my face, his touch infinitely gentle. "You are the most incredible woman I have ever known," he says with such intensity that tears spring to my eyes. "And you are going to be the most amazing mother."

"You can't know that," I whisper.

"I absolutely can," he counters. "I've seen you with children. I've seen how you fight for what's right, how you love without reservation, how you make everyone around you feel valued and heard. Our baby is the luckiest child in the world to have you as their mother."

A tear slides down my cheek, and he catches it with his thumb. "Hormones," I explain weakly.

"Of course," he agrees, not calling me on the obvious lie. "Now, tell me what you need. What can I do to help you through this?"

"Just stay with me," I say, suddenly overwhelmed by how much I love this man. "Be here."

"Wild horses couldn't drag me away," he promises, settling in beside me. "We're doing this together."

As if on cue, another contraction begins. Tristan helps me sit up, supporting my back as I breathe through it, murmuring encouragement in my ear. When it passes, he offers me ice chips, adjusts my pillows, makes sure I'm comfortable.

"Has anyone called my mother?" I ask suddenly.

"She's on her way," he assures me. "Should be here within the hour."

I nod, relieved. Despite our occasional clashes, I want my mother here for this momentous event. "And the press?"

"Kate is handling it," he says. "A brief statement that you've gone into labor, and updates will follow when appropriate. No details, no photographs, exactly as we planned."

Another wave of gratitude washes over me. Even in crisis mode, rushing to my side, Tristan remembered our careful plans for privacy during this intensely personal moment.

The next few hours blur together in a rhythm of pain and respite. Tristan never leaves my side, not even when my mother arrives and tries to convince him to take a break. The contractions intensify, and finally I agree to an epidural when the pain becomes overwhelming.

"You're doing beautifully," the doctor tells me during her next check. "Eight centimeters now. Not much longer."

Tristan wipes my brow with a cool cloth, his eyes never leaving my face. "You hear that? You're almost there."

I nod, too focused on the sensations in my body to form words. The epidural has taken the edge off, but I can still feel the pressure of each contraction, the inexorable movement of our child toward the world.

"I never thought we'd get here," I say during a brief respite. "When we first met, when you were this frustrating, arrogant prince who drove me crazy."

He laughs softly. "And you were the stubborn commoner who refused to be impressed by my title."

"Look at us now," I whisper, my eyes filling with tears again.

"Look at us now," he agrees, pressing his lips to my forehead. "About to be parents."

The word sends a fresh surge of panic through me. "Tristan, what if—"

"No what-ifs," he interrupts gently. "We'll figure it out together, just like we've figured everything else out."

Before I can respond, another contraction builds, this one with a different quality that makes me gasp. The doctor returns, checking me quickly.

"It's time," she announces, her calm voice cutting through my momentary fear. "You're fully dilated. On the next contraction, I want you to push."

Tristan's hand tightens around mine. "I'm right here," he reminds me. "Right beside you."

The next hour passes in a blur of pushing, breathing, and Tristan's steady encouragement. My mother stands by the door, her presence a quiet comfort, while Shannon waits outside. The medical team moves with practiced efficiency, their voices blending into background noise as I focus solely on bringing our child into the world.

"I can see the head," the doctor says finally. "One more big push, Your Majesty."

I gather every ounce of strength I have left, squeezing Tristan's hand so hard I'm sure I must be hurting him, though he doesn't flinch. With a final, monumental effort, I push—and suddenly feel the slippery sensation of our baby leaving my body.

A cry fills the room—strong, indignant, perfect.

"It's a girl!" the doctor announces, placing our daughter on my chest.

She's tiny and red-faced, covered in vernix, her little fists waving in protest at the bright lights and cold air. And she's the most beautiful thing I've ever seen.

"Oh my god," Tristan breathes beside me, his voice thick with emotion. "Lia, look what we did."

I can't speak, can barely breathe as I stare down at our daughter. Her eyes blink open—dark blue, unfocused—and I'm undone. Love crashes over me in a wave so powerful it's almost frightening, a fierce, primal need to protect this tiny person we've created.

"Hello, little one," I whisper, trailing a finger down her cheek. "We've been waiting for you."

Tristan leans over, his hand covering mine where it rests on our daughter's back. "She's perfect," he says, a tear sliding down his cheek. "Just like her mother."

The medical team moves in, asking if they can take her for a moment to clean her up and check her vitals. I nod reluctantly, already missing her weight on my chest the instant she's gone.

My mother approaches, her usual composure cracked by joy. "She's beautiful," she says, kissing my forehead. "You did wonderfully, darling."

Tristan doesn't leave my side, his eyes tracking our daughter as the nurses weigh her and wrap her in a blanket. "Six pounds, four ounces," a nurse announces. "A bit small, but perfectly healthy."

"Small but mighty," Tristan says with a proud smile. "Like her mother."

When they bring her back, placing her in my arms, I feel a completeness I've never known before. Our family, together at last.

"What shall we call her?" Tristan asks, perching carefully on the edge of the bed to gaze down at our daughter.

We'd narrowed it down to a few options, waiting to see which one felt right when we met her. Looking at her now—her tiny nose, the determined set of her chin that already reminds me of Tristan—I know immediately.

"Eleanor," I say softly. "Eleanor Grace."

Tristan's eyes light up. "It's perfect."

"Princess Eleanor Grace of Haldonia." I try out the full title, finding it suits her despite her diminutive size. "That's quite a name to grow into, little one."

"She will," Tristan says with absolute confidence. "With you as her mother, how could she not?"

A knock at the door draws our attention, and Shannon peeks in cautiously. "Is it safe to come meet the newest royal?"

"Get in here." I beckon with my free hand. "Meet your honorary niece."

She approaches, her usual efficiency melting into wonder as she gazes down at Eleanor. "She's gorgeous," she breathes. "Congratulations, both of you."

"Thank you for everything today," I tell her sincerely. "I couldn't have done it without you."

"Yes, you could have," she corrects me with a smile. "But I'm glad I was there."

The next few hours are a blur of visitors—doctors checking vitals, nurses offering guidance on feeding, Parker coming in briefly to secure the room before allowing a select few palace staff to offer their congratulations. Through it all, Tristan remains steadfast beside me, occasionally holding Eleanor with such careful reverence that it makes my heart ache.

As night falls and the room finally quiets, it's just the three of us. Eleanor sleeps peacefully in a bassinet beside my bed, Tristan stretched out next to me on the wide hospital bed, his arm around my shoulders.

"Are you all right?" he asks, studying my face in the dim light. "Really?"

"I'm exhausted," I admit. "Sore. Overwhelmed. And happier than I've ever been."

He pulls me closer, dropping a kiss on the top of my head. "You were magnificent today. I've never been more in awe of you."

"Even more than when I managed to navigate that diplomatic crisis with the Argentinian ambassador?" I tease, fighting to keep my eyes open.

"Even more than that," he confirms solemnly. "Today you brought our daughter into the world. Nothing will ever top that."

I glance over at Eleanor, watching the rise and fall of her tiny chest. "It doesn't feel real yet."

"It will," he assures me. "Probably around three in the morning when she decides it's time to eat again."

I laugh softly, careful not to wake her. "At least we have an army of nannies waiting at the palace."

"True," he agrees. "But for these first few days, I thought maybe it could just be us. The three of us, figuring things out together."

The suggestion touches me deeply. Despite the demands of running a country, despite the traditions and protocols that usually dictate our lives, Tristan wants these precious early days to be ours alone.

"I'd like that," I whisper, leaning my head against his shoulder.

As sleep begins to claim me, I think about the journey that brought us here—from reluctant royal bride to queen, from wary strangers to partners, from husband and wife to parents. None of it has been easy. Some of it has been downright terrifying. But all of it, every step, has been worth it.

Eleanor stirs in her sleep, making a tiny mewling sound that immediately draws both our attention. We watch, breath held, as she settles back into dreams, her perfect little face peaceful.

"We did good," I murmur, my eyes growing heavier.

"We did amazing," Tristan corrects me, his voice thick with emotion. "And this is just the beginning."

As I drift toward sleep in the arms of my husband, our daughter sleeping peacefully beside us, I can't help but think he's right. This isn't an ending—it's a beginning. The start of a new chapter in our story, one filled with new challenges and joys, fears and triumphs.

And despite the uncertainties that lie ahead, I know one thing with absolute certainty. As long as we have each other, we can face anything. King and queen. Husband and wife. Father and mother.

Family.

CHAPTER 28
TRISTAN

A soft cry penetrates my consciousness, pulling me from the light doze I've fallen into. My eyes snap open to find Amelia smiling down at our daughter, Eleanor, who's nestled in her arms. The sight still takes my breath away—my wife, my queen, holding our child. Our miracle.

"I think she's hungry," Amelia whispers, her voice tired but filled with so much love it makes my chest ache.

I check my watch. "The doctor should be here soon to discharge you both." I move to sit on the edge of the hospital bed, carefully placing my hand on Eleanor's tiny head. Her dark hair is so soft beneath my fingers. "I can't believe we get to take her home today."

"Me either," Amelia murmurs, leaning against me slightly. "I'm a little terrified, to be honest."

I press a kiss to her temple. "We'll figure it out together."

A knock at the door interrupts us, and Shannon pokes her head in. "Good morning, Your Majesties. I've brought everything for the queen to get ready."

"Perfect timing," I say, carefully taking Eleanor from Amelia's arms. "I have a diaper to tackle while you help my wife."

Shannon laughs as she enters with a garment bag. "Are you sure you don't want me to handle that, sir?"

"Absolutely not." I cradle Eleanor against my chest, marveling at how such a tiny human can command so much of my heart already. "The King of Haldonia changes his own daughter's diapers."

Amelia's laughter follows me as I make my way to the changing table set up in the corner of the private hospital suite. A nurse had shown me the basics yesterday, but this is my first solo attempt. I lay Eleanor down carefully, and she immediately begins to fuss.

"I know, princess," I murmur, keeping one hand gently on her chest while I gather supplies with the other. "Daddy's going to make this quick."

Eleanor's cry grows a bit louder, and I feel a momentary flash of panic. "It's all right," I say, more to myself than to her. "We've got this."

I unfasten the tabs on her diaper with what I hope is confident precision, though my hands feel too large and clumsy for such a delicate task. The nurse's instructions replay in my mind as I clean her, apply cream, and slide a fresh diaper beneath her.

"Almost done, little one," I promise as she wriggles beneath my hands. When I finally secure the tabs, I let out a triumphant breath. "There! Not bad for a first solo mission, right?"

"Looks perfect to me," Amelia says from across the room, where Shannon is helping her into a simple blue dress that will be comfortable for the journey home.

I scoop Eleanor up, pressing a kiss to her forehead before wrapping her in the soft blanket embroidered with the Haldonian royal crest—a gift from the prime minister. "Ready to see your kingdom, Princess Eleanor?"

"I just need five more minutes," Amelia says as Shannon helps arrange her hair into a simple style.

"Take your time. I'll go bring the car around to the private entrance." I carefully transfer Eleanor to Shannon's waiting arms. "Be right back."

Parker falls into step beside me as I exit the room. "Everything's secure, sir. We have the route cleared and teams positioned at both exits."

"And the decoy?" I ask, knowing the paparazzi will be waiting.

"In place. Though you should expect photographers at the main entrance as well. They've been camped out since news of the birth broke."

I nod, accepting this as part of our reality. "Let's get this over with, then."

When I exit through the main doors of the hospital to retrieve the Range Rover I insisted on driving myself, camera flashes immediately erupt from the cordoned-off area where the press waits. I raise a hand in acknowledgment but continue toward the parking structure.

"Your Majesty!" one of them calls out. "How does it feel to be a father?"

I pause, turning slightly. "Extraordinary," I answer honestly.

"You're setting a great example, bringing the car around yourself!" another shouts.

I manage a smile. "Just doing what any father would do."

The cameras continue clicking as I make my way to the Range Rover. Once inside, I take a deep breath, allowing myself one private moment before driving to the hospital's private entrance where Amelia and Eleanor will be waiting.

Parker meets me at the entrance, supervising as the hospital staff help Amelia into the back seat. Shannon carefully transfers Eleanor to the car seat we had installed and checked three times for safety. I watch like a hawk as they secure my daughter, making sure every strap is perfectly positioned.

Finally, Amelia squeezes my hand. "She's fine, Tristan. Let's go home."

I nod, closing her door before walking around to the driver's side. Parker takes his position in the security vehicle that will follow us, and I see him speaking into his radio, coordinating our departure.

As we pull away from the hospital, I glance in the rearview mirror to see Amelia watching our daughter with a mixture of awe and exhaustion on her beautiful face.

"You were incredible," I tell her, reaching back to squeeze her knee. "I'm so proud of you."

"We did it together," she says, though her eyes never leave Eleanor. "I couldn't have done it without you."

"That's not true, but I'll accept the compliment." I focus on the road ahead, keeping to the exact route Parker had planned. "Welcome to your first royal motorcade, Princess Eleanor."

"She's sleeping through it." Amelia laughs softly.

"Smart girl. Conserving her energy for when we get home."

The palace comes into view—home—and for the first time, I see it through new eyes. It's no longer just the place where I rule from. It's where our daughter will take her first steps, say her first words, grow up surrounded by love that my own childhood never knew.

"We're home," I say, my voice thick with emotion as I drive through the gates that open automatically for us.

Amelia's hand finds mine again. "The three of us."

I squeeze her fingers, overcome with gratitude for this family we've created. "The three of us," I repeat, as I park in front of our private entrance, ready to begin this new chapter of our lives together.

CHAPTER 29
AMELIA

The soft glow of the nursery lamp casts gentle shadows across the room as I shift Eleanor to my other breast, wincing at the sharp pain that shoots through me. Three days at home with our newborn, and breastfeeding still feels like an impossible challenge. The lactation consultant who visited yesterday assured me this was normal, that it would get easier, but right now, with my nipples cracked and sore and Eleanor fussing against me, I'm finding it hard to believe.

"Come on, sweet girl," I whisper, trying to help her latch properly. "I know you're hungry."

Eleanor turns her head away, her little face scrunching up in frustration before releasing a cry that seems impossibly loud for someone so tiny. Tears of frustration prick at my own eyes as I try once more to position her correctly.

"It's okay," I murmur, though I'm not sure if I'm talking to her or myself. "We'll figure this out."

The door opens quietly, and Tristan appears, his hair rumpled from the brief nap he'd been trying to catch between Eleanor's feedings. The circles under his eyes match mine, but the love in his gaze as he takes in the sight of us hasn't dimmed at all.

"How's it going?" he asks, crossing the room to perch on the arm of the rocking chair.

"Not great," I admit, my voice catching. "She won't latch properly, and it hurts so much, Tristan."

He reaches down to stroke Eleanor's cheek with his knuckle. "Maybe we could try the shield thing the consultant left?"

I nod, feeling a tear escape despite my best efforts. "It's in the basket by the changing table."

Tristan retrieves it and hands it to me, then kneels beside the chair as I position it and try again with Eleanor. This time, after a moment of resistance, she latches, and though it still hurts, it's bearable.

"There we go," Tristan says softly, his hand coming to rest on my knee. "You've got it, Lia."

I let out a shaky breath, relief washing over me as Eleanor began to suckle properly. "I thought this would be more…instinctive," I confess. "That I'd just know how to be a mother."

"Hey." Tristan's voice is gentle but firm. "You are an amazing mother. It's been three days, and you're recovering from giving birth while learning how to care for a tiny human. Give yourself some grace."

I lean my head against his arm, drawing strength from his presence. "When did you get so wise?"

"I've always been wise. It's part of my kingly charm," he says with a grin, and I can't help but smile back. "Speaking of kingly duties, I have that security council meeting in an hour."

My smile falters. "I forgot about that."

"I can cancel—"

"No," I cut him off. "You've already rescheduled twice. The country still needs its king."

Tristan sighs, running a hand through his already disheveled hair. "I hate leaving you both."

"It's just for a few hours," I remind him, though I'm dreading being alone with Eleanor, afraid I won't be able to comfort her if she fusses. "We'll be fine."

He studies my face for a moment, then nods. "I'll have Shannon check in on you, and I'll be back as soon as humanly possible."

"Try not to fall asleep during the meeting," I tease, remembering how he nodded off during a budget review in the final weeks of my pregnancy.

"No promises," he replies with a wink. "The Minister of Finance has a voice like a lullaby, and I'm working on about two hours of sleep."

As if on cue, he yawns widely, and I laugh despite my exhaustion. "Go get ready. Your country needs you conscious."

Tristan stands but lingers, watching as Eleanor continues to nurse. The look of pure adoration on his face makes my heart swell. "I still can't believe we made her," he whispers.

"I know," I agree, glancing down at our daughter's perfect little face, her dark eyelashes fanned against her cheeks. "She's the best of both of us."

He leans down to press a kiss to my forehead, then one to Eleanor's head. "I won't be long, I promise. If you need anything—"

"I'll call," I assure him. "Now go, before you're late and the prime minister sends a search party."

With visible reluctance, Tristan backs away toward the door. "I love you both," he says, his voice thick with emotion.

"We love you too," I reply, and the smile that spreads across his face is worth every moment of discomfort and uncertainty I've felt.

After he leaves, I finish feeding Eleanor, successfully burping her on my shoulder—a small victory that fills me with disproportionate pride. She's drowsy now, her tiny body heavy with milk and contentment. I carry her to the crib but find myself unwilling to put her down just yet.

Instead, I settle back into the rocking chair, cradling her against my chest as I breathe in her sweet newborn scent. Outside the tall windows, the sun is setting over the palace gardens, painting the sky in shades of pink and gold. In this moment, despite the exhaustion and the uncertainty, I feel a profound sense of rightness.

"Your daddy will move mountains for you," I whisper to Eleanor as her eyes flutter closed. "And so will I. You'll never doubt how loved you are, little one. Not for a single moment."

As Eleanor sleeps in my arms, I allow my own eyes to close, just for a moment. The weight of her against my heart is the most perfect anchor I've ever known, keeping me tethered to what truly matters in this life we've built together.

CHAPTER 30
TRISTAN

"Is her hat secure?" I ask for the third time as the car approaches the new Royal Haldonian Childcare Center. Through the tinted windows, I can already see the crowds gathered behind the barricades, eagerly awaiting their first glimpse of Princess Eleanor.

Amelia adjusts the tiny white bonnet on our daughter's head with practiced ease. "It's perfect, Tristan. Stop fussing."

"I'm not fussing," I protest, though we both know that's exactly what I'm doing. "I just want everything to be perfect for her first official appearance."

"She's one month old," Amelia reminds me with a smile. "She'll be perfectly happy as long as she's fed, changed, and in our arms. The rest of this"—she gestures toward the crowd outside—"is for them, not for her."

I know she's right, but I can't help the protective surge that rises in my chest at the thought of presenting our daughter to the world. For the past month, we've kept Eleanor mostly within the palace walls, sharing only a few carefully selected photographs with the public. Today marks her first real introduction to the kingdom she will someday help lead.

"You're right," I concede, reaching over to take Ellie—as we've taken to calling her—from Amelia's arms so she can gather her notes for her speech. Our daughter blinks up at me with her dark blue eyes, so trusting and content in my embrace. "You ready to meet your people, Princess?"

Ellie responds with a tiny yawn that melts my heart completely.

Parker opens my door first, scanning the area before giving me a nod. I step out, careful to keep Ellie shielded against my chest as the cheers from the crowd intensify. I turn back to offer Amelia my hand, and the sight of her emerging from the car sends another wave of applause through the gathered citizens.

In the month since giving birth, Amelia has found a new confidence that takes my breath away. She stands tall beside me in a simple blue dress that matches Ellie's outfit, her hair swept back in an elegant knot. The exhaustion of new parenthood is visible in the slight shadows beneath her eyes, but it does nothing to diminish her radiance.

"They love you," I murmur as we begin walking toward the red ribbon stretched across the entrance of the new daycare center.

"They love their princess," she corrects, smiling and waving to the crowd.

"They love their queen," I insist, knowing it's true. Amelia has captured the hearts of our people in a way my family never managed before.

The director of the center greets us at the entrance, curtseying deeply before leading us inside. The facility is state-of-the-art, designed to provide affordable childcare for working parents throughout the capital city. It's a project Amelia championed during her pregnancy, and seeing it come to fruition fills me with pride.

"Your Majesties, we're so honored by your presence today," the director says, guiding us through the brightly colored rooms filled with tiny tables, reading nooks, and play areas. "This center will serve over two hundred children, with priority given to single parents and families below the median income."

"It's exactly what we envisioned," Amelia says, her face lighting up as she takes in the details. "A place where children can thrive while their parents work without worry."

As we complete the tour, we're led to a small stage set up in the center's courtyard where the public ceremony will take place. Amelia steps up to the microphone first, while I stand slightly behind her, still cradling Ellie protectively against my chest.

"People of Haldonia," Amelia begins, her voice clear and strong. "Today we celebrate more than just the opening of a building. We celebrate a commitment to our children and to the parents who work tirelessly to provide for them."

The crowd falls silent, captivated by her words. I watch her with undisguised admiration as she continues.

"As a new mother myself, I have come to understand more deeply than ever before the challenges parents face. The sleepless nights, the constant worry, the impossible balance between work and family." She pauses, looking back at me and Ellie with a soft smile. "And I have been fortunate enough to have support at every turn. But not all parents are so lucky."

She turns back to the audience, her expression growing more passionate. "Every parent deserves to know their child is safe and nurtured while they work. Every child deserves the opportunity to learn and grow in a supportive environment. And every family deserves the dignity of being able to provide without sacrificing their children's wellbeing."

The applause that follows is thunderous. When it dies down, I step forward to join her at the microphone, carefully adjusting Ellie so that she's visible to the crowd while still secure in my arms.

"My wife, your queen, speaks with the wisdom that has always been her hallmark," I say, unable to keep the pride from my voice. "And as king, I am fully committed to supporting this initiative and expanding it throughout Haldonia."

I look down at my daughter, then back at the faces turned toward us—hopeful, expectant, trusting. "The future of our nation rests in how we care for our children—all of our children. Not just those born to privilege, like my daughter, but every child born within our borders."

After our speeches, we cut the ribbon together, Amelia guiding Ellie's tiny hand over ours as we do. The moment is captured by dozens of cameras, and I know it will be on the front page of every newspaper tomorrow.

As planned, we allow the public to approach in an orderly fashion, giving them a closer look at Princess Eleanor, who remains remarkably calm despite the attention. Many bring small gifts—handmade blankets, tiny stuffed animals, children's books—which Shannon collects to be sanitized and reviewed before they reach Ellie.

"She has your eyes," one elderly woman says to Amelia, who smiles graciously.

"And His Majesty's stubborn chin," adds another, drawing laughter from those nearby.

I pretend to look offended, which only increases the amusement. These moments of connection with our people are precious, reminding me why the sacrifices of royal life are worthwhile.

As the event winds down and we prepare to leave, I notice Amelia stifling a yawn behind her hand. Ellie is starting to fuss slightly, likely ready for her next feeding.

"Time to get our princess home," I murmur to Amelia, placing my hand at the small of her back.

She nods gratefully, giving the crowd one final wave as Parker escorts us back to the car. Once inside, Amelia immediately takes Ellie from me, checking her diaper before settling her into her car seat.

"You were brilliant today," I tell her as the car pulls away. "Both of you."

"She was perfect," Amelia agrees, pressing a kiss to Ellie's head. "Not a single meltdown."

"I meant what I said up there," I say, watching my wife and daughter with a fullness in my heart I never thought possible. "About expanding the program."

Amelia's eyes meet mine, hopeful but cautious. "The budget committee—"

"Will approve it," I finish firmly. "I'll make sure of it."

Her smile is worth every political battle I'll have to fight. "Thank you, Tristan."

"No," I say, leaning over to press my forehead against hers, creating a small circle with our daughter between us. "Thank you for showing me what truly matters in this kingdom."

As we drive back to the palace, I watch the city pass by outside the window, seeing it now through the eyes of a father, not just a king. The responsibility feels heavier than ever, but so does the purpose, the clarity of what I'm fighting for.

For Ellie. For Amelia. For all the families who depend on us to lead with compassion and vision.

For the future we're building together, one day at a time.

CHAPTER 31
AMELIA

The gentle creaking of the rocking chair fills the nursery as I sway back and forth, Ellie nestled against my chest. Her eyes are heavy with sleep, but she fights it, tiny fists opening and closing against my night-gown as she stubbornly tries to stay awake. Just like her father, I think with a smile, always resisting rest when there's more to experience.

Tomorrow marks my official return to royal duties—my first full schedule of engagements since giving birth six weeks ago. While I've maintained certain responsibilities from home and made the appearance at the daycare center, tomorrow signals a true return to the balancing act of being both queen and mother.

My stomach twists with a mixture of anticipation and anxiety. I press my lips to Ellie's downy head, breathing in her sweet scent, trying to memorize this feeling of her warm weight against me. Will she miss me? Will I miss some important milestone while sitting through a meeting? Am I making the right choice?

The soft click of the door interrupts my spiraling thoughts. Tristan enters carrying a tray, moving with the careful quiet that we've both mastered over the past few weeks of parenthood.

"I thought you might need reinforcements," he whispers, setting the tray on the small table beside the rocking chair. I see two steaming mugs of hot chocolate topped with whipped cream, and a bowl of ice cream with chocolate sauce drizzled artfully over the top.

"Comfort food?" I ask, raising an eyebrow.

He shrugs, a boyish smile playing at his lips. "I figured you could use it. Pre-first-day-back jitters and all."

"How did you know?" I shift Ellie slightly to accept the mug he offers.

"Because I know you," he says simply, settling into the armchair across from me with his own hot chocolate. "And because I heard you pacing in here for the last hour."

I take a sip of the rich chocolate, feeling warmth spread through me. "I'm being ridiculous, aren't I?"

"Not at all." His expression grows serious. "It's a big step, going back."

"I keep telling myself that women do this all the time," I say, glancing down at Ellie, whose eyelids are finally beginning to flutter closed. "Return to work, leave their babies with capable caregivers, continue with their lives."

"True," Tristan agrees, leaning forward. "But that doesn't make it easy. And most women aren't also the queen of Haldonia."

I laugh softly. "There is that small detail."

He sets down his mug and moves to perch on the ottoman beside my rocking chair, close enough that I can see the flecks of gold in his brown eyes.

"Lia," he says softly, using the nickname only he is allowed. "You know you don't have to do this yet, right? If you want more time, it's yours. No one would question the queen taking a longer maternity leave."

The offer is tempting—more mornings watching Ellie's face light up when she sees me, more afternoons spent singing to her as she kicks her legs during tummy time, more evenings like this, rocking her to sleep while the world carries on without us.

But there's something else pulling at me, too. A responsibility that extends beyond the walls of the nursery.

"I want to do this," I say, surprising myself with the conviction in my voice. "I need to."

"Why?" Tristan asks, not challenging but curious, wanting to understand.

I take a moment to find the right words. "Because I want to be the kind of queen our people can relate to. A woman who loves her child fiercely but who also has ambitions and responsibilities beyond motherhood." I look down at Ellie, now sleeping peacefully against me. "I want her to grow up seeing that it's possible to be both—a mother and a leader."

Tristan's eyes shine with understanding and something deeper—pride, perhaps. "You're remarkable, you know that?"

"I'm terrified," I admit. "What if I can't do it all? What if I fail at both?"

"Then we'll figure it out together," he says, reaching for the bowl of ice cream and offering me a spoonful. "That's what partners do."

I accept the bite, savoring the cool sweetness as it melts on my tongue. "Partners," I repeat. "Not exactly what we signed up for when our parents arranged this marriage, is it?"

Tristan laughs quietly. "Not even close. I was expecting a political alliance at best, constant warfare at worst."

"And instead?" I prompt, already knowing the answer but wanting to hear him say it.

He takes the empty mug from my hand and sets it aside, then reaches out to brush a strand of hair from my face. "Instead, I found the love of my life and the mother of my child. I'd say we got extraordinarily lucky."

"We did," I agree, feeling the truth of it settle deep in my bones. This arrangement that once filled me with dread has become the greatest blessing of my life.

Ellie stirs against me, her little body completely relaxed in sleep. "I think she's finally out," I whisper.

Tristan stands, holding out his arms to take her. "Let me put her down."

I transfer our daughter carefully, watching as Tristan cradles her with practiced ease, pressing a gentle kiss to her forehead before laying her in the crib. He stands over her for a long moment, his face softened with love in a way that still makes my heart skip.

I join him, sliding my arm around his waist as we both gaze down at our sleeping daughter. "She looks so peaceful," I murmur.

"She has no idea she's a princess," Tristan says with wonder in his voice. "No idea the weight that comes with that crown."

"We'll help her carry it," I promise. "We'll make sure she knows she's loved for who she is, not what title she holds."

Tristan turns to face me, taking both my hands in his. "Just as I love you for who you are, not because you're my queen."

"And I love you for the man you are, not because you're my king," I reply, leaning into him. "Who would have thought an arranged marriage could turn into this?"

He wraps his arms around me, pulling me closer. "The best diplomatic arrangement in Haldonian history," he murmurs against my hair.

I laugh softly, careful not to wake Ellie. "We should tell our diplomats to try it more often."

"No," Tristan says, pulling back to look into my eyes. "What we have is rare, Lia. A love match disguised as a political necessity. I don't think lightning strikes that way twice."

The conviction in his voice makes my chest tighten with emotion. "Then I guess we got extraordinarily lucky," I whisper, echoing his earlier words.

"Beyond lucky," he agrees, his forehead coming to rest against mine. "And tomorrow, when you step back into your royal duties, I'll be right beside you, just as I've been here with you through these first weeks with Ellie."

"Partners," I say again, the word now carrying the weight of a vow.

"In parenting, in ruling, in everything," Tristan confirms. "Always."

As we stand together beside our daughter's crib, the moonlight streaming through the window illuminates the three of us—a family created from duty but sustained by love. Tomorrow will bring new challenges, the delicate balance of motherhood and monarchy, but tonight, in this perfect moment, I know with absolute certainty that we will face it all together, stronger for the unexpected love we've found in each other.

EPILOGUE
TRISTAN

THREE YEARS LATER

"Don't wake your mom up," I tell Ellie as she and I are quietly making our way around the bedroom.

Lia is pregnant again. Something we weren't sure we wanted, but in the end, we let nature take its course, and here we are. We haven't found out the gender, but I'm convinced it's a boy based on her morning sickness being much worse this time. We haven't told the people of Haldonia yet, but Ellie and our friends know.

"Tired?" Her head tilts to the side.

"Yeah, Mama's tired. Come on."

She puts her small hand in mine, and together we toddle down the long hallway to the dining room. Parker and Shannon are already there, laughing. When they see us, Parker bends at his knees and holds his hands out.

"Ellie, good morning!"

Her small hand lets go of mine, and she runs to where he is, letting him pick her up easily. "Park!"

She can't say Parker yet, but she makes her presence known all the time. "Lia is still asleep," I say, glancing over to Shannon. "Let her.

She's been tired lately. I'm gonna take Ellie with me." I look up at Kate. "Can you rearrange my schedule?"

"Will do." She grins down at Ellie. "Wanna go get some breakfast?"

My daughter nods with all the enthusiasm of a child who knows she's about to get sugary cereal, and there's nothing her parents can do about it. "I'm going to go check on Lia, and then I'll be right back," I tell them after we finish most of our coffee and breakfast. Getting up from the table, I walk through the palace but stop at the sitting room. Lia is standing there, looking at a picture of my mother. Quietly I walk in. "Are you okay?" I whisper, putting my arms around the stomach that's growing faster this time.

"Yeah," she sighs. "I just wonder. Would she have liked me?"

My throat tightens slightly. "She would love you just as much as I do."

Her body sinks into mine, and right here in this moment, the kid who wondered if he'd ever find love after the one person who gave it unconditionally was gone, knows without a doubt he's found it. Love. Pure, simple, and everything he's dreamed of.

In fact, we've rebuilt a country on it.

A LOOK AT: TEMPTED
GRIZZLY RIVER RANCH BOOK ONE

Some lines should never be crossed… but men like this are worth the risk.

When Aubree Weber returns to Grizzly River Ranch in South Dakota heartbroken and pride bruised, the last person she expects to fall for is Jesse Nelson. Her brother's best friend. Her former protector. Her former protector. The cowboy who kissed her on her eighteenth birthday… then walked away.

Now twenty-seven and reeling from a failed relationship, Aubree can't ignore the way Jesse watches her across the ranch. He's no longer the safe, steady boy she once knew. And when she catches him sneaking off with his brothers, stealing cattle for their own operation, she sees just how dangerous he's become. His threat should scare her. Instead, it lights a fire she thought had died.

With her brother Truett, the only family she has left, injured in a ranch accident, Aubree is forced to rely on Jesse. The man who once pushed her away now looks at her with raw hunger. And when he finally admits he's tempted, she realizes she's been playing with fire.

Loyalty runs deep on the ranch, and secrets can destroy everything. If Aubree falls for Jesse, she risks the only family she has left. But some cowboys don't ask permission—*they take what they want.*

AVAILABLE DECEMBER 2025

Laramie Briscoe is the *USA Today* and *Wall Street Journal* bestselling author of over thirty books, with sales of over half a million copies.

Since self-publishing her first book in May of 2013, Laramie has appeared on the Top 100 Bestselling E-books Lists on Amazon Kindle, Apple Books, Barnes & Noble, and Kobo. Her books have been known to make readers laugh and cry. They are guaranteed to be emotional, steamy reads.

When she's not writing alpha males who seriously love their women, she loves spending time with friends, reading, and marathoning shows on Netflix. Married to her high school sweetheart, Laramie lives in Bowling Green, Kentucky, with her husband (the Travel Coordinator) and an adorable dog named Gus.

www.laramiebriscoe.net